A Mysterious Girl

Danny glanced over his shoulder again and there was the girl, hugging Jordan even tighter, if that was possible. She was talking and laughing. Her beautiful hair was blowing in every direction. She looked so comfortable with her arms around Jordan. And yet, this morning Allison had been so comfortable with Jonathan.

That made Danny realize there was something different about Allison. . . .

Her clothes, Danny realized. He was sure that Allison had been wearing a red-and-orange sweater this morning. But now she had on a blue sweater. That was strange, Danny thought.

It was yet another strange thing about this very strange girl.

NEW KIDS ON THE BLOCK™: The Novels

The Novels

NEW KIDS ON THE BLOCK

Between Brothers

R. Paul Yockey

AN ARCHWAY PAPERBACK
Published by POCKET BOOKS

New York London Toronto Sydney Tokyo Singapore

The names Jordan Knight, Jonathan Knight, Joseph McIntyre, Donald Wahlberg, and Daniel Wood and their individual likenesses are used with permission of the individual artists and Big Step Productions, Inc. This book is a work of fiction. Except for the artists comprising NEW KIDS ON THE BLOCK no similarity between any of the names, characters, persons and/or institutions in this book with those of any living or dead person is intended and any similarity which may exist is purely coincidental.

AN ARCHWAY PAPERBACK *Original*

An Archway Paperback published by
POCKET BOOKS, a division of Simon & Schuster Inc.
1230 Avenue of the Americas, New York, NY 10020

Packaged by March Tenth, Inc.

NEW KIDS ON THE BLOCK®, NEW KIDS® and NKOTB®
and related indicia are trademarks of Big Step
Productions, Inc. and are used only with permission.

ISBN: 0-671-73941-7

First Archway Paperback printing September 1991

10 9 8 7 6 5 4 3 2 1

Cover art by Keith Birdsong

Printed in the U.S.A.

IL 6+

Chapter

1

JORDAN KNIGHT didn't see the taxi rounding the corner. But then, Jordan had forgotten he was crossing a street. Fortunately, Jordan was walking with his brother.

"Look out!" Jonathan yelled. He grabbed Jordan by the collar of his brown leather jacket and jerked him backward. Jonathan had a way of knowing when his brother was in trouble.

Brakes squealed, horns blared. A hoarse voice shouted in a foreign language, and water was splashing everywhere. The yellow taxi shot past. The driver, who had a blue turban wrapped around his head, shook his fist angrily.

As they reached the curb, Joe ran up to the brothers and said, "Jordan, are you okay?"

"No prob," said Jonathan, shaking the muddy water out of his black hair.

"What were you thinking about, anyway?" Joe asked.

"He was thinking about those cute girls standing under the awning of that deli," said Jonathan. "You don't expect Mr. Romeo to care about a little old taxicab when there are girls around, do you?"

Jordan gave Jonathan a friendly shove on the shoulder. It was at times like this he was glad to have his big brother as a fellow member of the New Kids on the Block.

"Next time warn me *before* I get in trouble, man."

"What for? No way you're gonna listen. I warned you not to wear your favorite jacket in the rain, but you didn't listen."

Looking down, Jordan saw the dark splash across the front of his brown aviator jacket. He had chosen it just to look his best for the big photo session with *Teen Rhythm* magazine.

"Oh, great."

"You've got more jackets than anybody I know," Jonathan said. "You had to wear leather in the rain."

"Hey," Joe said with a grin, "the original owner probably wore it in the rain a lot."

"And that's no bull!" Jonathan shot back. *"Hawr-hawr-hawr!"* His loud laugh startled a young man who was rolling up the awning with a long metal pole.

The rain stopped as suddenly as it started. The two girls moved away down the street. They were unaware that they had very nearly been the cause of an accident. They had no way of knowing that they had been checked out by one of the famous New Kids.

"New York is probably the only city in the USA where the New Kids on the Block can walk around without being noticed," Joe said.

"Let's just see if we can get where we're going without running into any more taxis," Jonathan chimed in. "Donnie and Danny will be waiting for us."

3

"Not to mention Dick Scott," said Jordan. Their business-minded manager hated anyone being late for an appointment.

"Dick said he'd have our hides if we showed up late this morning," Jordan added.

"Well, we'll just give him your cowhide jacket, Jordan," joked Joe. He slapped Jordan on the shoulder of his prized jacket. "Unless the wet-cow look is part of your new fashion statement!"

At a midtown office building Allison Holtz heard the elevator bell ring. Someone was getting off at the *Teen Rhythm* floor. Allison looked up from the copying machine and saw three people walking down the hall.

Allison recognized two of the group as members of the New Kids on the Block. She guessed that the third, a bald-headed black man, was their manager.

The smiling-faced boy was obviously Donnie. She was surprised to hear him speaking with great concern about some homeless people he had seen on their drive into the city.

From what Allison heard on the local

radio talk shows, the New Kids were not the kind to think about anything but food, girls, and music. Not that she believed everything she heard on the radio, of course.

Still, with the New Kids arriving for big concerts at Madison Square Garden, there were an awful lot of rumors going around about the boys. You couldn't turn on the radio without hearing another wacky story.

"They say Danny eats nothing but raw hamburger and bean sprouts," one kid told a deejay. Another caller asked if it was true that the circus was being canceled because of the New Kids concerts.

Now here's this one member of the group, Donnie Wahlberg, talking like a real person, Allison thought. I guess you really can't believe everything you hear.

Allison Holtz was known as a "gofer" around the *Teen Rhythm* offices. She was an intern, learning the ropes while she finished school. She would "go fer" lunch, "go fer" coffee, "go fer" the newspapers—whatever anybody told her to do.

But this was closer than most girls her age got to the entertainment business.

That was the business Allison wanted to be in. Her ambition was to be an actress on the Broadway stage. Allison worked hard to balance her acting lessons with work, not to mention trying out for every part that came along in the theater.

Maybe she would meet someone at the magazine who could give her a start in show business, just as she had read about in novels and seen in the movies.

Allison was finishing up at the copying machine when the elevator bell rang again. Then she heard the sound of talking in the hallway. She picked up her copies and stepped into the hall, right into the arms of Jonathan Knight.

"Whoa! You okay?"

"Sorry, I didn't realize you were—"

"That's okay. Here, let me help you."

Jonathan bent down to help Allison pick up some of the papers that had gone flying. She noticed his dark eyes and long lashes. The front of his hair was still wet, and it smelled like rain. The back of his hair was messed up, as though it had been covered by the hood of the all-weather jacket he was wearing.

"I'll bet you had this all collated—every page in order, right?"

"It's okay, really."

"That looks like a pretty fancy copier. Maybe we could just feed the pages back in or something. I'm pretty good with machines."

At that moment Joe broke in, saying they did not have time to check out the workings of a copy machine. People were waiting for them.

Jordan agreed. "Maybe you've forgotten, but we have got a whole day of picture-taking ahead of us."

Jonathan said he was sorry he couldn't stay to help. Allison said that was okay. Jonathan smiled and gave a little wave as he turned to leave. Allison waved back, watching the boys go through the big glass doors to the main editorial offices of *Teen Rhythm*. What they did not know was that Allison had been making copies of their schedule. It was six pages long. The New Kids on the Block would be seeing a whole lot of New York City before their three days of photo sessions were over.

"Hey, guys, you missed a great breakfast," said Donnie as the latecomers entered the office. "Dick took us to this amazing bagel place. You can have bagel sandwiches with eggs and anything else you want on them."

"Even tofu," said the health-conscious Danny.

"Gross," Joe barked.

"Of course, Donnie had a garlic bagel with ham and salami and egg and peanut butter and—"

"We get the picture," said Jordan. "Where's Dick?"

At that moment their manager, Dick Scott, came into the reception area with three women. One of them was Allison, carrying a set of blue-covered production schedules. Ahead of her came a short woman carrying cameras.

The leader of the group ushered Dick in and made a great fuss over her guests. She was a tall, thin black woman with a streak of gray in her long hair. She spoke in a deep, musical voice that made her sound as though she came from some exotic foreign country.

"So, thees is the famous New Keeds! It is quite an honor, I must say."

The tall woman wore glasses shaped like stop signs that sat near the tip of her narrow nose. Her flowing dress was printed in a bold red-and-yellow flower pattern. It was caught up at the middle with a belt of wooden beads. Her costume made her seem like some African princess.

She went from one to the other, taking each boy's right hand in her two hands as she introduced herself.

"You are Mr. Wood, to be sure," she said, shaking Danny's hand and patting it. "Very muscular. I am Shakamabe Tosulu."

Next she found Jordan. "And Mr. Knight, the dancing composer. Please call me Shaka."

Jordan made a little bow to her. It seemed like the thing to do.

Moving to the oldest of the New Kids, Shaka said, "The other Mr. Knight, Jonathan, is it not? I shall need your help, no doubt. We must keep these other young men from losing themselves in the wonderful sights of New York City."

She put her hands on her hips as she came to Donnie. "Mr. Wahlberg. So pleasant to meet you. We shall speak of politics together, I hope." Donnie smiled broadly.

Finally Shaka wrapped her long,

ringed fingers around Joe's hand. She pressed it firmly and Joe could not help thinking of his grandmother. However, Shaka did not look *anything* like Joe's grandmother.

"And, of course, Mr. McIntyre. You must stay close by me so I can tell you many things about this amazing city. Some call it Gotham. Some call it the Big Apple. Shaka calls it *home*."

Shaka turned with a little spin. It made the skirt of her dress wrap around her long legs. Her every movement seemed like a part of some long-ago dance.

"Let me introduce you all to Miss Monica Merriweather," she said. "Monica will be our photographer. For the next three days she is the boss, okay? When Monica says, 'Jump,' the New Keeds say, 'How high, Miss Merriweather?' You dig me, yes?"

"We've got you covered, Shaka," answered Jonathan.

Monica was a chunky young woman. She smiled to show a row of teeth outfitted with the latest in bright red braces. They sparkled like Christmas ornaments.

Monica Merriweather was loaded down

with camera equipment. Bags hung from both shoulders, with long lenses strapped to their sides. Around her waist was a belt covered with loops that held rolls of film. They looked like bullets in the old-time Western movies.

Monica wore baggy pants and a baggy jacket. Both had lots of pockets and zippers. She seemed to poke out in unexpected places, like some old toy bunny rabbit that was losing its stuffing.

"Let's get cookin', buddy-buddies," Monica said. Her voice was clipped and sharp, but her Christmas-tree grin gave it a pleasant feel. "Lots of f-stops to check and rolls of celluloid to spread with sunshine."

Jordan had no idea what the woman was talking about, but he didn't care. His attention was focused on the third member of the *Teen Rhythm* crew. He looked at the pretty girl with the papers. She was the one that Jonathan had nearly run over in the hallway. She had spectacular eyes.

"And who is this?" he asked.

"Oh," said Dick Scott, looking up from his notebook. "This is Allison."

"Allison Holtz," said Allison.

"Chillin'. And will you be coming along with us?" asked Jonathan.

"I don't think—"

"Hey, Shaka's gonna need some help showing us around," said Jordan.

Allison looked from one brother to the other with her huge brown eyes. "But I have work to do around here," she said.

Shaka put her arm around Allison and said. "It perhaps is time you get some experience in the field, yes? You will take notes and keep us on schedule."

A worried look crossed the girl's face as she handed out the schedules. She said she would love to go along, but her expression said something else.

"Okay if I make a phone call before we get started?" she asked.

"Most assuredly," answered Shaka, "so long as it is a brief one. Now, anyone who requires freshening up, please do so. Return here for departure in five minutes."

Jonathan and Jordan stood before the long mirror in the men's room, combing their hair.

"This place is like the United Nations," Jordan said. "That Shaka is awesome.

And how about the cabdriver with the turban—where do you think he came from?"

"From around the corner, you dweeb. *Hawr-hawr-hawr!*" Jonathan could not resist the joke.

"Yeah, yeah," said Jordan. "But, like, I want to see some foreign places while we're in New York City, you know? Like Little Italy and Chinatown. Like that restaurant where all the big shots go, the Russian Tea Room. That's where I'm gonna take that five-foot factor called Allison."

Jonathan stopped combing his hair and frowned at the reflection of his brother in the mirror. "Hey, step off, Jordan. I saw her first. If anybody's taking Allison to the Russian Tea Room, it's me."

"You saw her like you saw that taxi driver. Oops, excuse me!"

"I mean it, Jordan. You make dates with half the girls you see, and you see most of them. Allison's special."

"You bet she is, Jon, and that's why *I'm* taking her to dinner."

The two reflections in the mirror were glaring angrily at each other now. Fortunately, they were joined by a third reflection, that of Joe. He elbowed his way in to wash his hands.

"Like, I can't believe this," Joe said. "Bill and Ted's excellent argument. Two knights jousting over the same fair damsel."

That brought a smile to Jordan's face, but Jonathan still had a serious look as he turned to leave.

"Let's break," he said.

"Outta here," Joe said, drying his hands on his jeans. "You know, I still haven't told the taxicab story to Danny and Donnie. 'Course, I'll have to add a few facts of my own, just to make it funnier."

As they followed Jonathan down the hallway, Joe noticed that the water splash on Jordan's leather jacket was fading away. "Of course, you never know," he said. "It might leave a ring, like when you sat the soda bottle down on my mom's good dining room table."

"Chill, Joe. Let's go spread some sunshine on the celluloid."

"Oh, right. Whatever that means."

Chapter

2

DANNY LOUNGED IN THE BACK of the New Kids' tour bus, sipping an icy fruit drink. Outside the tinted windows Manhattan's East Side rolled by. Ordinarily, Danny would have been checking out the amazing New York sights. Instead, he was watching the action in the front of the bus.

He could hardly believe it. Jonathan and Jordan were acting like a couple of first-timers with this girl Allison. What *is* it with these guys? he wondered.

In the front of the bus Jonathan had the aisle seat with Allison by the window. Jordan propped himself up on the railing,

15

facing Allison. He was doing his best to distract her attention from Jonathan.

Samantha, the driver, kept telling Jordan to go find a seat. Jordan ignored her at first. Then he said he would go in just a minute. Then he said all right, he would leave. Then he'd move away for a couple of seconds and bounce right back again. All the while he kept breaking up Jonathan's conversation with Allison.

"So, like, have you lived here all your life?" Jonathan was asking.

"Well," Allison answered, "we moved from Mississippi when I was real little. Maybe a few months or something. My dad works on building ships, and he got a job in Brooklyn, so that's where we live."

"Brooklyn?"

"Yeah."

"Say," Jordan broke in, "I remember the last time we came to New York we played in that old movie theater in Brooklyn. It used to be a movie theater, only they made it into a college gymnasium. You know the one?"

"It used to be the Brooklyn Paramount, Jordan," Jonathan cut in. "But Allison was talking about *her*."

"So? Chill, bro."

Samantha shot an angry look at Jordan. "You still standing there?"

"Sam, everybody's on my case today. Nobody loves me. Boo-hoo."

Jordan pretended to wipe away tears. Grinning broadly, he walked toward the rear of the huge bus, which was actually their home on wheels when they traveled from city to city. Suddenly Jordan began to make up a song:

> "Nobody don't love me,
> They're all on my case.
> Like a one-legged runner,
> 'Bout to lose the human race."

Joe reached up and grabbed a stuffed gorilla from an overhead rack. He sent it flying through the air toward the back of Jordan's head.

But Jordan grabbed the toy gorilla before it hit him in the side of his face. He held it up with one hand, still singing. His "instant lyrics" never skipped a beat:

> "Tryin' to swing through the jungle
> With monkeys on my back,
> Tryin' to get to you, baby,
> But my train's run off the track."

Then Jordan swung into his bunk and pulled the curtain closed.

Danny did not think for a moment that Jordan had given up on Allison. Now that Danny thought about it, this was the first time he had ever known the brothers to go riffin' on each other like this. You could count on Jordan to posse up with Jonathan. And Jonathan was always cool to his little brother. This Allison must be some happenin' lady. Danny took a big sip of his fruit drink.

"Say *Gorgonzola*."

Danny pulled away from the straw with his cheeks puffed out like a chipmunk's, full of icy fruit freeze. His eyes went wide just in time to have a camera flash go off and blind him.

"Say *what?*" Bubbles sputtered from Danny's mouth just as the flash went off again.

"Great shot!" exclaimed Monica Merriweather. "I think I got that goop splashing out right into the lens. Great stuff."

"Say *what?*" Danny repeated, wiping his face with his painter's cap.

"Say *Gorgonzola*," the little photographer smiled. Her red braces lit up almost as bright as her camera flash. "That's my favorite kind of cheese. What's yours?"

"Feta," said Danny. "That's Greek goat cheese. It's healthier for you."

"Shoulda known," said Monica, moving off toward the front of the bus. "Hey, there's the U.N."

Shaka, the *Teen Rhythm* editor, was pointing it out to Joe and Donnie. The long, low building was almost completely surrounded by waving flags. Reds and blues and yellows and greens—the colors waved and flapped together like one long quilt.

"All these countries in one place," Shaka said. "Just like New York City, you see. People from all the world come together. Here you know it is true when they say we are all brothers and sisters."

"Sometimes we don't act like brothers and sisters, though," Donnie said. He and Joe looked at each other with serious expressions, and then they both looked toward Jonathan in the front seat.

Jonathan was getting pretty serious himself, serious about Allison. He had his legs propped up on the railing that led to the front door of the bus. He was telling Allison what a good time they would have at the party after the concert tonight.

"I can really go backstage?" Allison asked. Her big brown eyes were wide with delight.

"Guaranteed," Jonathan promised. "Just watch out for the roadies."

"Roadies?"

"The guys that put up all the lights and the sound gear and stuff. They travel everywhere ahead of us, so they're called roadies. They're cool but kind of rough. Not the Allison type."

"That sounds like a . . . like, a compliment?" Allison was not sure.

Suddenly they were interrupted by a low-pitched voice: "Yo, dude. What's happenin'? Is this a smokin' ride or what?"

Allison was startled to see a character in a yellow trench coat with a long beard, a duck-billed cap, and giant sunglasses standing in the aisle. Doing a breakdance slide and half-spin, this strange person stepped down to lean against the front of the bus.

"Strange things are afoot at the Circle-K," he growled. This was Jordan in one of his many disguises, but Allison didn't know that.

At just that moment the bus hit a huge pothole and bounced up hard. The bearded man lost his balance and fell headfirst across the handrail. He landed in Jonathan's lap with his arms around Allison's neck.

Allison opened her mouth to shriek but got a mouth full of beard. Jonathan accidentally hit the armrest button that caused his seat to lean back.

That's when the little voice of Monica Merriweather chirped, "Say *Gorgonzola!*" and the flash went off.

"Jordan, you are totally wacked!" shouted Jonathan.

"Jordan?" asked Allison, definitely surprised.

"Well, it's not Santa Claus or Abe Lincoln," growled Jonathan, pulling off his brother's fake beard and sunglasses. He gave Jordan a shove that sent him sprawling into the aisle.

"Take a walk off the back of the bus, Jordan."

"This bus is stopping," said Samantha. "You have arrived alive at the world-famous World Trade Center."

21

Allison looked at her watch and said, "I've gotta get to a phone."

Donnie pointed out the window. "There's Biscuit and Bud," he said.

The two bodyguards were standing nervously on the plaza between the two towers of the World Trade Center. Biscuit, the big, burly man, was shifting from one foot to the other. Bud stood tall and blond and stiff, only his eyes darting back and forth behind their shades.

"I can't believe it," said Joe. "Eleven A.M. and still no screaming fans."

"Out, cheeldren," said Shaka in her husky voice. "It is a long ride to the top floor."

With the crazy photo schedule Shaka had for them, the boys knew they had no time for autograph-hungry fans. So Biscuit split them up into two groups for the ride up the elevator to the World Trade Center's 110th-floor observation deck. They would be less noticeable that way, he said.

Danny found himself on the elevator with Jonathan and Allison. He watched how the girl moved, talking with her hands and giving little shakes of her head. Her soft, nut-brown hair moved like leaves in a gentle breeze.

It was no trick to see why Jonathan and Jordan both were falling for her. Allison could speak about art and drama, about music and movies. These were the things Jonathan liked.

At the same time she was very cute and very sweet. That made her just the type for Jordan.

What bothered Danny was the trouble Allison was causing. She was driving a wedge between Jonathan and his brother Jordan. Something like that could ruin the spirit that held the New Kids together.

Danny was determined not to let anything happen that might break up the group. But he did not want to break up a good thing between Jonathan and Allison, either. The more he thought about it, the more confused Danny became.

"I guess this is where we get off," Jonathan said when the elevator came to a stop.

Danny noticed that Allison was gripping his hand.

"I've never been up this high before," she said.

23

"Hey, maybe this is halfway to heaven," said Jonathan.

"Sounds like a new song title," Danny remarked as he ushered the lovebirds out of their nest. "Me, I could use some food."

"Yogurt at thirteen hundred feet," joked Jonathan. "We'd better hook up with the others and get the shots laid down."

"I'll get you something, Danny," Allison offered. "I need to find a phone, anyway. The sign over there says there's a snack bar one level down."

"That'd be great," Danny answered. "I'm starved."

"Don't worry," Allison said, ducking into a stairway. "I'll be back in a few minutes."

"Cool lady," Danny said to Jonathan after Allison had left.

"Oh, *yeah*," Jonathan agreed. "And I think, you know, I think she digs me for *me,* you know? Not just because of the New Kids."

"What's her thing with the phone?" Danny asked.

"She won't say. Says she's gotta check in at home."

Just then Danny remembered something. "Hey, I've gotta go find Allison. I didn't give her any money for the food. I better go catch her. You posse up with the gang, and I'll be right there."

In a minute Danny was down the stairs and scanning the snack bar for Allison. He found her just where he knew he would, at the pay telephones. As he waited for her to finish, Danny could not help overhearing Allison's conversation.

"I know it's a lot to ask," she was saying. "But if you just help me out this once. You know what he's like."

What *who's* like? Danny wondered. Jonathan, maybe?

"He already told me I had to choose between my job and him. He'll never give me another chance if I blow this one. He says this time I'm the girl, the only one."

This was getting very interesting. Danny couldn't help himself. He leaned closer to the wall of telephones.

All at once Danny realized he was surrounded by a troop of Girl Scouts. They were whispering and giggling and pointing.

"Say, aren't you . . ."

"No way!"

"Bet he is."

"Oh, *really*."

Danny felt himself breaking out in a cold sweat, the way only a stampede of wild girls could make him feel. As calmly as he could, he pulled out a stick of gum and began to unwrap it.

Backing toward the stairway, he began to chew. The Girl Scouts were edging closer. What was their motto, Danny tried to remember. "Be prepared"? No, that was the Boy Scouts. "We always get our man"?

"Danny!" one of them screamed.

Suddenly there was a wall of green jumpers, pigtails, and award badges flying at him. He pulled the stairway door shut behind him and bounded up the stairs three at a time.

Danny's heart was pounding as he ran out on the observation deck. On every side there were tourists posing for pictures, with the skyline of Manhattan behind them. Biscuit and Bud, the bodyguards, were gazing across the Hudson River through large coin-operated binoculars mounted on a stand.

Where were the New Kids?

There! He spotted them on the south side of the building. Monica Merriweather was posing them with the Statue of Liberty in the background.

"Yo, Danny," called Donnie. "Where you been?"

"They're after me," Danny puffed. "Little green women."

All at once the stairway door burst open and out poured dozens of Girl Scouts, shrieking and charging.

"Danny!"

"Jon!"

"Joe!"

"Donnie!"

"Jordan!"

"New Kids!"

There was no escape. By the time Biscuit and Bud arrived, the girls had them surrounded. The New Kids were autographing everything that would hold ink.

"These will make great photographs for our story in *Teen Rhythm!*" shouted Shaka in a commanding voice.

Monica Merriweather had her motordrive camera clicking and whirring away. She bobbed and weaved as she took picture after picture, searching for just the right angle.

Soon the New Kids realized what was happening, and they all burst out laughing. They stopped trying to escape the scouts. They posed for pictures with them and pretended to dance with them as Joe played air guitar. They spun the big binocular machines around and climbed up on them. Pretty soon they knew all the girls by name.

"Where are you from?" Joe asked.

"Indiana," answered a redheaded girl with freckles and a face-crinkling smile. "A town called Lebanon."

"We won a trip to New York by selling the most Girl Scout cookies," said another girl. She was snapping a photo of Donnie with his arm around the redheaded girl. Meanwhile, Monica Merriweather was snapping a photo of *her*.

"Yo, did somebody say 'cookies'?" Donnie asked in a voice loud enough for all to hear. "I could go for a few chocolate chips right about now."

"There's a snack bar one floor down," said Danny. That made him think about Allison. Was she still on that telephone?

"No time for food now," said Shaka. "Lunch will be after our next stop. Time to go."

As they told the Girl Scouts goodbye and packed into an elevator, Jordan asked, "Where is our next stop, anyway?"

Shaka laughed. "Do you not read those careful schedules I make out?"

"Nah," said Jordan.

"Hey, wait a minute," Jonathan interrupted. "Speaking of schedules, where's Allison? Stop the elevator."

"No way," rumbled Biscuit, anxious to keep the New Kids moving along. "This here's an *express* train. We're not stopping until we get to floor number *one*."

"Yeah, but Allison—"

"Do not worry, Jonathan," Shaka said. "We will continue on, and she will catch up. She has a schedule, too, you know. And she knows how to buy a subway token."

"I don't like the idea of her all alone in this big city," Jonathan argued.

"Really now," said Shaka. "Allison makes her way around this big city just fine every day, with no help from New Keeds."

They climbed into the bus. Sam already had the engine revving and ready to roll.

"Don't worry, Jonathan," said Jordan. "Allison will be attracted back to us by my magnetic personality."

"You wish," grumbled Jonathan, pushing his way onto the bus ahead of Jordan.

Danny watched with growing concern. Jordan would keep trying to joke and Jonathan would keep taking him seriously. Usually, the Knight brothers thought just alike. They were just like those twin towers of the World Trade Center.

As they took their seats, Shaka passed out shiny red apples, two for each New Kid.

"But you are not to eat them," cautioned Shaka.

"How come?" asked Donnie.

"Just put them in your jacket pockets," said Shaka. "You are about to meet some friends who will like these apples *very* much."

Joe was studying his schedule. "What's up about this next stop, Shaka? It just says Garden. What kind of garden do you bring apples to?"

"The Garden of Eden," said Jonathan. "*Hawr-hawr-hawr.*" He glanced toward his younger brother across the aisle. Jordan looked at him but did not return the smile. He looked mad.

That stopped Jonathan's laughter.

"No," said Shaka, "not the Garden of Eden. In Manhattan the most famous garden is Madison Square Garden."

"That's where our concerts are gonna be," said Joe.

"Tonight, the New Keeds show," Shaka agreed. "But before that, 'The Greatest Show on Earth.'"

Chapter

3

THE BUS PULLED UP next to a police barricade along a wide, busy street, and the New Kids stepped off. They were led inside a large building and through a series of hallways until they came to a large open area that looked like the inside of a huge barn. There they were surprised to find themselves looking at a line of swaying elephants.

"Gentlemen," Shaka announced, "meet the Proud Pachyderms of Kingsley Brothers Circus. I think they are even beeger stars than the New Keeds, yes?"

"What are they here for?" asked Donnie.

Shaka smiled. "They are here for you."

"What are we gonna do with a herd of elephants?" Joe wanted to know.

"You are going to ride them, Joseph," answered Shaka.

"*Ride* them?"

"Whoa!"

"Awesome!"

"Ride them *where*?"

"To the truck yards," said a small brown man with a high-pitched voice. "To the docks on Twelfth Avenue. You must think of them as a crosstown bus, my friends."

"These will make wonderful photographs for our *Teen Rhythm*, no?" asked Shaka. Then she looked at the man.

The little man grinned at Shaka, showing a set of sparkling white teeth. His bald head and pointy beard gave him a comical look. He was dressed in a red jacket with two gold buttons, brown shorts, and old sneakers. He carried a long stick with a hook on one end.

"Mehli Singh!" said Shaka.

33

"Shakamabe Tosulu!"

The little man and Shaka embraced. She was so tall she seemed to wrap him up in her flowery dress. It was plain that they knew each other.

Standing on tiptoe, the man called Mehli kissed Shaka on each cheek.

"Well, how is this for elephants, I would like to know?" Mehli asked.

"For elephants this is very fine, Mehli." Shaka leaned back and put her hands on her hips. "Very fine for elephants! I thought you might get me one or two elephants, but I see five."

"No-no-no-no-no," Mehli said, shaking his head rapidly. He looked and sounded a bit like a corn popper. "You see six. That is, you do not see number six, because he is standing behind his mother, which is number five."

Just at that moment there was a toot like a toy trumpet. The baby elephant pushed his way between two enormous adults, raising his trunk for attention.

"That is Jee-Jee," said Mehli. "You told me five New Kids, so I get five elephants. But Miss Grisette," he said, pointing to one of the elephants, "she must bring along her own new kid, don't you know."

"Hawr-hawr-hawr!" Jonathan enjoyed the joke, especially after the tense bus ride.

Danny interrupted the conversation of the two old friends. "So, Shaka, we gonna, you know, climb up their trunks or what?"

"Mehli," said Shaka, "you can explain it all to them. But first I make the introductions, yes?"

Shaka introduced the New Kids to Mehli. She said that she and Mehli had met in Sierra Leone, the part of Africa where she was born. Mehli's family came from India.

"I am so pleased to make the acquaintance of you," Mehli said. "Now you must meet the rest of my present family. You brought with you some little presents, I trust?"

The New Kids looked puzzled. Then Shaka said, "The apples."

They all dug in their jacket pockets for the shiny red apples and came out with one in each hand. All except Danny. He produced one apple and one apple *core*.

Joe smirked. "Yo, very rude Dan. Better put Danny on that baby elephant."

"He's for the baby New Kid," Danny

shot back, laughing. "That is definitely a Joe McIntyre-size elephant."

"No, I got it," said Jordan. "Let's give Nikko a ride on the baby elephant." Nikko was the sharpei dog who often accompanied the boys on their road trips.

"Oh, yeah," Jonathan added. "Nikko's got more wrinkles than any three of those elephants."

"And he doesn't eat half as much as garbage-can Dan," said Jordan.

That brought a loud *Hawr-hawr-hawr* from Jonathan. The noisy laugh set two of the elephants to trumpeting. Nikko started barking inside the bus.

Danny laughed, too. He was glad to see the Knight brothers joking together again, even if the joke was on him.

Shaka produced more apples from her enormous leather handbag, and the whole party moved over to where the elephants waited. Mehli began to explain the fine points of elephant riding.

"The elephant will kneel down for you to mount," he said. "You may put your foot on his knee and swing your left leg over. You may grab the ear where it meets the head and pull yourself up by that.

36

This will not be abusive in the least to the elephant."

"Don't we get saddles or anything to ride on?" asked Donnie. He had seen elephants lots of times at the Boston Zoo, but he had never ridden one.

"No-no-no-no-no! Most especially not necessary," said Mehli. "Sit please just behind your elephant's head, and you will discover yourselves most comfortable. You will find a rope there for holding on, but nothing else is necessary, to be sure. Hold on with your legs and your knees, that is all."

Monica Merriweather started taking pictures like crazy as the boys were introduced to their elephants. One by one each New Kid met an elephant. When Danny held his hand out, his elephant curled its rough trunk around the apple and lifted it to its mouth. The boys patted the trunks of the elephants and felt the strange, rough skin.

"It feels kind of like the tread of a car tire," Danny remarked.

"More like a slice of leftover pizza that's been in the back of the fridge for a couple of weeks," said Donnie. "Only not cold, you know?"

"The skin is very thick," said Mehli. "That is what the word *pachyderm* means. So we call elephants 'pack-i-derms.' Of course, you knew that long before."

"Oh, right," said Joe.

Every elephant had a name and seemed to know when Mehli spoke to it.

Danny's elephant was Omara, Donnie had Kusu. Jonathan got Barbie, and Jordan got Liz. Joe would ride the elephant called Miss Grisette. Mehli shook his head and waved a finger at the idea of Nikko riding Jee-Jee, the baby elephant.

"Not safe," he said. "The cherished pet may all too easily fall underfoot and become treaded upon. Most unpleasant to contemplate."

"Sharpei pancake," Joe grimaced. "Definitely uncool."

Just at that moment Shaka gave a little shriek. Something was tugging at her purse. When she looked down, there was Jee-Jee, the baby elephant, digging with her trunk in the big bag.

"Purse-snatching pachyderm," joked Jordan. "Call the cops."

BETWEEN BROTHERS

"Most unnecessary," said Mehli. He gave the little elephant's trunk a tap with his long stick. "I have the curious suspicion that Miss Tosulu has brought along something good to eat."

The little trunk came out of the bag. The pink tip of the trunk had a very tight grip on an apple.

Shaka laughed as the baby elephant chewed the apple to a pulp. Juice dribbled down its chin.

"Jee-Jee needs a bib," Joe said.

Soon, with the help of Mehli and his assistant trainers, the boys mounted their elephants. Of course, Monica Merriweather was snapping away with her camera just as Danny swung himself up. And, of course, Danny swung just a bit too hard. He went sliding down the other side of the elephant.

"Whoa!" Danny shouted. He landed with a soft thud on a bale of hay. "I thought you said Omara was a gentle one."

"Omara is as gentle as her trunk is long, Daniel," said Mehli as he rushed over to help. "It is your mighty leap that is not gentle."

"Hang tough, Danny!" shouted Jordan, high up on Liz's back.

"This is definitely *not* happenin'," Danny complained. He walked around Omara for another try.

At that moment, the TV crews arrived. With portable lights, cameras, and lots of other equipment, they prepared to videotape the New Kids' spectacular ride through the streets of New York City.

Just then, Allison appeared.

"I'm sorry I missed the bus!"

Allison was just the person Shaka needed at that moment.

Shaka looked around and saw the trainers bringing their elephants to a standing position. Only Jordan Knight's elephant was still kneeling. She shouted to Mehli that there was a second passenger for that elephant.

"All right, camera people," Shaka called to the TV crews. "We have a good shot for you. Please step over here."

The camera crews had been standing on the other side of a police barricade, but now they hurried over to where Shaka and Allison stood. Shaka reached into her purse and pulled out a little notepad and

40

a pencil. She handed the pad and pencil to Allison.

"Here," Shaka said, "Now you are a *Teen Rhythm* reporter, yes? Go get on that elephant with Jordan."

She led Allison to the elephant as the cameras began to roll.

"As you know, ladies and gentlemen, the New Kids are here for photos for *Teen Rhythm*. Miss Allison Holtz is one of our reporters, and she will be riding along as the boys get this very unusual tour of New York City. Miss Holtz will be happy to talk with you at the end of the ride. However, I am afraid we will have to rush the New Kids along to their next appointment."

Shaka smiled as she watched the TV camera people videotape Allison being helped onto the elephant by Mehli. Allison would be the only female in the pictures and would no doubt be the envy of every *Teen Rhythm* reader.

The cameras were rolling as Jordan reached down and put his arm around Allison. He was helping her up onto the elephant, and that would make a very nice picture, Shaka thought.

41

Slowly the parade began its march through the streets of New York City from Madison Square Garden to the West Side truck yard. Monica Merriweather darted around the elephants, bumping into the TV crews, determined to get the best shots.

High above the street, swaying to the gentle rhythm of Liz's pace, Jordan felt Allison's arms around his waist. If he closed his eyes, he could imagine they were riding through the jungle together. In the distance he could hear the roar of lions and the beat of native drums.

"Me Tarzan. You Jane," he said.

"No," said the firm voice in his ear. "You Jordan. Me, uh, Allison."

"That's cool with me," Jordan answered. "Allison, I've been thinking about being alone with you all morning. I just never imagined it would be like this."

"That makes two of us," the girl answered.

"Like somebody said in a song, hang tough."

"You mean, hang *on,* don't you? If I'm bruising your ribs, I'm sorry. This is scary."

42

"Squeeze just as tight as you want to," Jordan answered.

From his own elephant Danny waved to the crowds on either side of the street in front of them. All along the way, bright orange police barricades blocked off the street to regular traffic. Right behind him was Jordan's elephant. Danny stopped waving and looked at Jordan and Allison sitting together high on Liz's back. Boy, he thought, Allison sure has a tight grip on Jordan.

On the next elephant, following Jordan, came Jonathan. Danny noticed the frown on Jonathan's face as he waved to the people on the sidewalks. Jonathan just couldn't help watching as his brother put the moves on Allison. And yet there was absolutely nothing Jonathan could do about it.

Danny began to wonder what was going to happen at the concert tonight. Would the Knight brothers be able to put aside their differences and perform together? He certainly didn't want the concert to be ruined.

Danny turned his head and saw people everywhere. People gathered in small groups at office windows. People waved from the sidewalks. Everyone stopped to watch as the little parade went by.

"Who's that?" some of them would ask.

"That looks like the New Kids on the Block," somebody would answer.

I should be having a good time, Danny thought. I should not be worrying about Jonathan and Jordan. I mean, how many guys ever get to ride an elephant across Manhattan? This is truly a bodacious ride!

Danny soon became thirsty, and that made him think of lunch. It was going on 2:00 P.M. and still no lunch.

Danny glanced over his shoulder again, and there was the girl, hugging Jordan even tighter, if that was possible. She was talking and laughing. Her beautiful hair was blowing in every direction. She looked so comfortable with her arms around Jordan. And yet this morning Allison had been so comfortable with Jonathan.

That made Danny realize there was something different about Allison. She had seemed so worried this morning when she talked on the telephone. Now she was happy and relaxed. There definitely was something different about her this afternoon.

Her clothes, Danny realized. He was sure that Allison had been wearing a red-and-orange sweater this morning. But now she had on a blue sweater. That was strange, Danny thought.

It was yet another strange thing about this very strange girl.

The elephants ambled along, trunk-to-tail, behind their police escort. The TV crews and Monica Merriweather would speed ahead in their cars, then jump out and take more pictures. Then they sped ahead to another location. It was like a game of leapfrog played by cameras and elephants.

Finally they reached their destination at the docks. Big trucks awaited their arrival. Some were already filled with the other circus animals.

The trainers had the elephants kneel to allow the New Kids to get off their backs.

Danny gave Omara a scratch behind the ear before he slid down to the ground. His elephant had become like a friend in the ride across the island of Manhattan.

Donnie patted Kusu and talked to her. Standing on the ground, he dug in his pockets and found a piece of a candy bar left over from a snack in Pittsburgh. He gave the candy to his elephant, and the animal gobbled it up.

Joe hugged Miss Grisette's trunk. "I wish you could come with us," he said. "You and your baby, too. I don't think Nikko would mind."

Only Jonathan and Jordan paid no attention to their mounts, Barbie and Liz. Jordan was too busy helping Allison off the elephant. Jonathan was too busy watching Jordan help Allison. As soon as Allison's feet touched the ground, Jonathan hurried over to her.

"So we're having lunch together, right, Allison?" he asked.

The girl looked up, her hand in Jordan's. She seemed surprised to see Jonathan.

"I, well . . ."

"Too late, Big Brother," said Jordan, unable to resist a smirk. "This lady's having lunch with me."

46

Jordan and Allison turned and walked toward the bus. Jordan waved at the TV reporters, who were begging for an interview.

Jonathan couldn't believe this was happening to him.

Chapter

4

As THEY WALKED to the tour bus, Jordan and Allison were discussing where they would go for lunch. Jordan had his heart set on the Russian Tea Room. It was a famous fancy restaurant right in the middle of Manhattan, and Jordan wanted to show Jonathan he could handle a place like that.

"How about the Hard Rock Cafe?" Allison suggested. "They have pictures of you on the walls there."

"Yeah," Jordan replied. "Also a thousand kids looking for autographs. Let's go somewhere more private for lunch."

Biscuit met them at the door of the bus.

"I know the perfect place for lunch," he said. "It's really cool. It's got a great view of Manhattan. It's got real cozy seats, music, and all your friends will be there."

"What kind of food does this place serve?" asked Allison.

"Well, this place has everything you could want—overstuffed deli sandwiches, sodas, potato chips, and pickles."

"But we don't want sandwiches," said Jordan.

"Just what is this place?" asked Allison.

"This place is *this place*," said Biscuit. He grinned and made a deep bow, waving them into the bus with a sweep of his arm.

"Give me a break, Biscuit," Jordan complained.

"Hey, ain't my gig, man. Dick Scott called on the radio. He said to get my boys done with that photo business and back to the hotel so they can get ready for their show.

49

"I told him you haven't had lunch yet. Dick said feed 'em on the bus while they drive to the next setup. I'm feedin'. You eatin?"

"It's cool, Jordan," Allison said. "Really. After all, what girl wouldn't die for a chance to eat lunch on a bus with all the New Kids on the Block?"

"She's right, Jordan," said Jonathan, stepping up onto the bus. "What girl wouldn't die for a chance to have lunch with *all* the New Kids?"

The bus rolled back down to the tip of Manhattan Island, where the gang would catch a ferry to the Statue of Liberty. As Danny wolfed down his special sandwich of bean sprouts on Middle Eastern bread, he found himself watching the romantic triangle once again.

This time it was Jordan who held the girl's attention and Jonathan who tried to distract her. On the last bus ride Allison had seemed artistic, sensitive, and totally attracted to Jonathan. Now she was the opposite, chattering away to Jordan. Danny couldn't figure it out.

Then he remembered that phone call. Who was Allison calling? And who was that guy she was talking about on the phone? The guy who told her she was "the only one"? *Who* might not give her another chance?

Was that guy *Jonathan*, as Danny had thought at first? If this girl was crazy about Jonathan, she sure had a strange way of showing it.

Maybe there was some other guy in her life. But then why was she flirting with Jordan? Danny didn't get it, not at all.

They seemed like one big happy family again as the bus bounced along the bumpy New York City streets. Jonathan clowned with Nikko, making the little dog hop across the aisle, from one seat to another, to catch a bite of beef brisket.

Allison thought Nikko was *"sooo cute!"* —which was just the reaction Jonathan was hoping for. Joe and Donnie got into the act with Nikko, playing a game of fetch that had all the markings of a food fight. There was nothing Jordan could do except play along. After all, if this was what Allison enjoyed, it was cool by him. Still, there had been something appealing about a quiet little table at the Russian Tea Room.

"So Alli," Joe said. Joe gave everyone a

nickname. "You comin' to the concert tonight or what?"

"I wouldn't miss it for anything," she squealed. "I got my tickets the day they announced you guys would be here. I had to stand in line three hours at the ticket counter in Macy's. By the way, is there any way I could see you when the show is over?"

"Are you kidding?" Joe blurted out. "Yo, Jon, didn't you tell this girl about backstage passes?"

Jonathan looked up, puzzled. He was rubbing the wrinkles on Nikko's belly, making his back legs kick the air.

"Well, yeah. I mean, don't you remember, Allison? I said there'd be a pass waiting for you."

"Oh, cool," Allison said. "I, uh, just must have been thinking about something else when you said that."

"Like me, maybe?" Jordan gave a big laugh that sounded just the tiniest bit like one of his brother's *Hawr-hawrs*.

Donnie felt the urge to change the subject before the Knight brothers got into a real argument. He asked Biscuit where they were meeting up with Shaka.

"On the ferryboat," he answered. "They got a ferry that takes you out to the Statue of Liberty. Shaka's meeting with the captain or somebody. She's making sure they can take us right out and bring us back in a hurry."

"I think there's a place to freshen up at the ferry landing," Allison said. "I hope you can wait a few minutes for me."

"Hey, we got everything you need right on this bus," Biscuit said, pointing to the bathroom at the back of the bus.

"That's okay, Biscuit," said Allison, "but I'll just use the rest room at the landing."

Danny looked over at Donnie and saw the trace of a frown cross his face and quickly disappear. Danny figured he wasn't the only one who noticed something peculiar about this girl.

The sandwiches and chips were hardly gone when the bus pulled into the ferry landing. "Everybody out for Ms. Liberty," called Samantha the driver.

They all piled out of the bus and headed up the ramp to the ferryboat. Allison excused herself and disappeared into the ladies' room.

53

Shaka met the New Kids with a security guard who ushered them through a turnstile gate. Shaka told the boys to hurry because the boat was about to leave the dock.

"I have been talking with the captain," she said. "He has given us permission to take a few photographs in the pilothouse, but we cannot all go."

"A house for airline pilots?" asked Joe.

"Hawr-hawr-hawr," laughed Jonathan. And just at that moment the ferryboat horn went off. It sounded very much like Jonathan's laugh, but maybe just a little bit louder.

"The pilothouse is where the captain steers the boat," Shaka explained. "You want to steer the boat, Joseph?"

"Joe?" Donnie exclaimed. "No way. We'll end up in, like, Cuba or someplace."

"Okay," said Shaka, "then *you* will steer the boat, Donnie. Danny, you go along, too. With Monica and her cameras there is not much room in the pilothouse, so I will return below in a moment."

Shaka disappeared with Donnie and Danny up a set of metal stairs. The ferry was crowded with tourists, most of them trying to get to the top deck so they could snap photos of the famous statue. Joe, Jon, and Jordan were happy to stay below.

"Sometimes it's really nice," Jonathan commented, "when you're *not* the center of attention."

With another blast of its horn the ferry pulled away from the dock. Biscuit looked back at the city as the boat churned out into the chilly waters of New York Harbor.

Biscuit gave a little shiver and said, "I don't much care for boat rides. Only thing worse is an airplane."

"Don't worry, Biscuit," said Joe. "I don't think they're really gonna let Donnie drive this thing. At least, I hope not."

"Really. We'll be in *big* trouble if they do!" said Jordan. "But no problem, 'cause look at all these handy life preservers."

"Got one big enough to fit around Biscuit?" asked Jonathan. *"Hawr-hawr-hawr!"*

"Hey, wait a minute!" Jordan exclaimed. "We left Allison back at the dock."

"Naw, she must have followed the other guys up to the pilothouse," said Jordan.

"First she follows Jonathan, then she follows Jordan," said Joe. "Now she's following Danny and Donnie? Maybe she'll take to following *me* next, huh?"

"Oh, yeah. Right," said Jordan.

Shaka rejoined the boys and took a seat on the bench.

Jordan said, "Did you leave Allison with the other guys?"

"No, I thought she was with you! Oh, dear," said Shaka with a concerned voice. "I very much fear our girl has missed the boat."

"She sure missed the boat with Jonathan this morning," said Jordan, giving his brother a thin-lipped smile.

"You probably chased her away, man. You came on *way* too strong!"

"Boys, boys," cautioned Shaka. "I seem to detect a sibling rivalry here. Don't forget that Allison has a job to do."

"I don't know," said Jordan, shaking his head. "Sometimes she seems like two different girls."

"Well, perhaps she is," said Shaka.

Jonathan looked surprised. "What do you mean?" he asked.

"Well, in a way, Allison is trying to be two different people." Shaka folded her long fingers and brought her hands up to her chin.

"You see, on the one hand she must work and finish school, because that is the course her father has set her on. Yet, on the other hand Allison has her own heart set on becoming an actress. So she is trying to be two women at the same time, and that is very hard."

"She really wants to be an actress, huh?" asked Joe.

"Oh, yes. And from what I hear," Shaka continued, "she just might have the talent to be one." Then Shaka turned away to see to some last-minute details.

"Maybe that's what's going on here," Joe said when she was gone. "Maybe this girl's trying to use the New Kids as a free ride to Hollywood."

"You mean, maybe her falling for us is just an act?" Jonathan asked.

"If it is"—Jordan shrugged—"that does make her a pretty good actress."

"I don't buy it," said Jonathan. "No

way. This morning it was like Allison and I were made for each other. Then, this afternoon, she was hanging all over Jordan like that dumb leather jacket of his."

"Hey, back off, Jonathan. Just because she doesn't care for you doesn't mean she has no taste."

Meanwhile, Danny and Donnie were taking their turns posing at the wheel in the pilothouse. They tried on the captain's cap for Monica's camera, clowning as she snapped away. The Statue of Liberty grew larger and larger as they got nearer.

Monica stopped to change film and the boys turned the wheel back over to the captain. He was a red-faced man with a white beard and a thick mustache.

"You're doing fine," the captain told them. "Five minutes at the wheel and we still haven't broken up on the New Jersey rocks. You must be from a seafaring town."

"Boston," said Danny.

"Aha!" the captain shouted. "See there, I knew it. There's another famous harbor in Boston."

"Really!" Donnie laughed. "We've been

to the New England Aquarium, if that counts."

The captain went back to his work, using a telephone receiver to bark orders to someone in the engine room. Danny took the opportunity to ask Donnie how he felt about Allison.

"She's pretty cool, I guess," Donnie answered. "But I have a feeling that's not what you want to know."

"Right. I'm worried about Jon and Jordan."

"Me, too," Donnie said. "We've all got pressures on us, being this close all the time. But maybe it's harder on them, you know, being brothers."

"Yeah. I mean, I used to think that it was easier for them because they were used to being together all the time. Now I'm not so sure." Danny looked confused.

"I know what you mean," said Donnie. "You can pick and choose who your friends will be, but with relatives it's different. You get born into a family, and you have no choice."

"Yeah," Danny continued. "Brothers and sisters are supposed to be friends from day one, whether you really like each other or not."

"Right. But there's another side to it," said Donnie.

"What's that?"

"Like, always wanting your brother to succeed," Donnie explained. "Like wanting him to have the best science project and be the fastest runner, just because he's your brother."

"Like, brotherly love."

"Yeah."

The ferry eased into the dock at Liberty Island, and the New Kids reassembled on the lower passenger deck. All the tourists were pressing together, to be the first ones off.

"So, Shaka, are we going to climb up to the Statue of Liberty's crown?" asked Joe.

"I'm sorry, Joseph, but there is no time for playing the tourist. I promised Dick Scott I would have you boys back to the hotel in plenty of time to get ready for tonight's concert.

"We need just a few more shots in that grassy area. Monica can take pictures of New Keeds just having a good time, with the Statue of Liberty in the background."

"How can we 'pretend' to have fun? All

work and no play is rotten," Jonathan sulked.

"It's just like you to complain," answered Jordan.

"What do you mean? I never complain," Jonathan raised his voice to his brother.

"Hey, you two! What's the big deal? Cool it. Let's posse up and show these cameras the New Kids spirit." Danny put his arm around Jordan and Jonathan and led them to the grassy area.

"You're right, Danny. Let's get out of this brother-against-brother gig and get real." Jordan looked over to his brother with a smile.

"Yeah," Jonathan agreed. "Let's practice that new routine for tonight's concert. I'm in the mood to groove."

Jonathan and Jordan danced over to the base of the statue, ready for the *Teen Rhythm* camera. Danny was glad that Allison seemed to be out of the brothers' minds.

Chapter

5

BACKSTAGE, deep in the heart of the huge arena, the boys could hear the band tuning up. The sound technicians were running their last sound checks. The roar of the crowd was beginning to build.

Joe McIntyre was running around switching everybody's hats. He pulled an aviator's cap off Jonathan's head and stuck on a kind of squooshed-up black hat with a narrow brim.

"What do you call that?" Jonathan asked.

"This here hat is called a porkpie. I mean, really, Jon baby, this hat is *you.*"

"Cool!" Jonathan grinned, admiring himself in the mirror.

"Joe knows hats," said Joe.

Lugging a duffel bag filled with hats, he moved over to the couch, where Jordan was pulling on his boots. Joe pulled the Boston Red Sox cap off Jordan's head.

"Yo, man! Definitely un-cool to wear a Red Sox cap in New Yaw-uk," he exaggerated in his best Brooklyn accent. Joe dug into the bag and pulled out a Yankees cap.

"No way," said Jordan, slapping away the emblem of the Red Sox's hated rival.

"All right, then, I got the perfect solution." He reached down into the bag and came up with a blue cap. On the front was an elaborate orange letter.

"What's this?" asked Jordan.

"An *M*" Joe replied, "for the New Yaw-uk Mets."

"Oh, yeah," said Jordan. "That's that team in the other league. They don't play Boston. I can handle that."

Donnie and Danny walked into the dressing room, loaded down with flowers. It was the same story everywhere the New Kids played—dressing rooms full of flowers.

"Anybody here named McIntyre?" Danny kidded. "All these here funeral arrangements are for Mr. Joseph McIntyre."

Donnie had a rose in his mouth and tried to joke through his clenched teeth. "Nobody sends me no flowers. Nobody don't love me. I'm gonna eat me a worm."

"Give it a break, Donnie," Jordan begged.

Dick Scott poked his head in the door of the dressing room. He had a walkie-talkie next to his ear, in communication with the stage manager and the lighting director.

"Everybody ready?" Dick asked.

"Almost!" shouted Donnie, picking up a hair dryer to give his hair one final touch.

"Let's move it," Dick Scott insisted. He pulled the hair dryer from Donnie's hand and placed it back on the table. Then he gently pushed Donnie forward.

The arena was rocking with the cheers and foot-stomping of the New Kids' fans. They seemed to sense that the magic moment was almost at hand.

All at once the amplified voice of an announcer blared above the noise of the crowd:

"La-deez and gen-tul-men . . . welcome to the world's most famous arena . . . Madison . . . Square . . . *Garden!*"

The crowd erupted into a frenzy, and the band began to play their long introduction to the first song.

"Posse up," Jonathan said.

Out in the hallway, leading to the ramp that would take them onstage, the boys formed a huddle. Arms draped around each other's shoulders, they shared the secret ritual that bonded them as a group.

They began each concert in this way, but tonight there was something special about the huddle. Danny could feel the melting away of tension between the Knight brothers.

"Okay," Jonathan said. "As of this moment we lay aside any garbage that's been bugging us. The problems no longer exist. We are one."

Jordan looked him straight in the eye. "One," he said. "No more problems."

"Okay," said Joe. "Let's go show these

New Yawkuhs what this place was built for."

The boys broke their huddle with a cheer. Danny felt that at last their troubles really were behind them. Then a flash went off.

"Oops, I forgot to say, 'Say *Gorgonzola!*'" It was Monica Merriweather. And standing next to her was Allison Holtz.

"Allison," said Jordan and Jonathan at the same time.

"You made it!" Jordan continued.

The two brothers walked up to Allison. Together they kissed her, one on each cheek. She seemed amazed at all the attention.

"You didn't think I'd miss this, did you?" she asked.

"Well," said Jonathan, "you sure missed that ferryboat this afternoon."

"Pay attention, guys. Here we go," said Dick Scott.

Jordan pulled Jonathan into line as the announcer's voice called out above the roar: "And now . . . the New . . . Kids . . . on . . . the *Blo-ock!*"

Once again the spotlights waved and fake smoke filled the stage. Laser lights danced in a frenzy of popping colors. The concert was on!

It was a lively audience, the kind of audience that usually makes for a great show. The New Kids really got into the music.

Halfway into "The Right Stuff," Danny felt so good that he improvised on one of the dance routines. As the rest of the kids moved together, Danny did a flying somersault and rolled to the edge of the stage into a handstand. The crowd went wild.

During a break between numbers, Jordan leaned over to Joe and said, "These kids must all be Mets fans. I can't believe an audience this cool would go for the *Yankees*. Let's bring 'em back to Boston, huh?"

"Show 'em how we do it up in Beantown!" Donnie yelled.

Joe gave a high-pitched whoop and threw a fist into the air, as if to say, "Right on!" Jonathan slapped him a high five.

The band began to play the next number. It was a slow, romantic song called "I Believe in You," and it started with a solo by Jordan:

"I believe in you
Every little thing you do . . .
Every time we kiss, it always feels like
  this
I believe in you."

As he sang, Jordan noticed a girl pushing her way to the front of the crowd on
the arena's floor, almost to the edge of the
stage. He was surprised when he recognized the girl as Allison.

She was supposed to be backstage, but
there she was out front, screaming and
waving as hard as any other fan. Well,
Jordan would just sing this love song to
her:

"Maybe I might sound crazy
For the way I feel about you,
But, baby, you're just so amazing,
And I'm so in love, girl . . ."

Jordan cupped the microphone close to
his lips and pretended to be kissing Allison. He whispered the final words of the
song, pointing to Allison as he sang:

". . . with you.
I believe in you."

68

As the saxophone player took off on a solo, Jordan smiled and blew a kiss. The girls in the audience standing near Allison went crazy, realizing the kiss was meant for her. They began to hug Allison, as though to congratulate her for receiving this special attention from one of their favorite New Kids.

It was plain to Jordan that he was the reason for the smile on Allison's face. It made him feel good. Not that he wanted to rub it in, but he had to admit there was something distinctly cool about beating out his older brother with this girl.

Jonathan wasn't watching. Maybe he didn't even realize that Allison was out in the audience. There's a lot my big brother doesn't know, Jordan thought, allowing himself a smug smile.

As the sax solo came to an end, Jordan whipped the baseball cap off his head and threw it right to Allison. She gave a little shriek as she caught it. The girls around her seemed to just fall apart.

Later, as the show ended and the New Kids ran offstage dripping wet from their workout, Jordan stopped and looked back into the audience. He didn't see Allison in the sweeping spotlights, but he knew she was there.

Jordan also did not see his brother.

As Jonathan came offstage, he took off his funny hat to mop the sweat off his forehead. There was Allison, standing behind the sound system with Monica Merriweather.

Monica was snapping off shots, and Allison was applauding wildly. Jonathan had the feeling she was cheering just for him. In a moment of inspiration he tossed the porkpie hat over Monica's head, right into Allison's outstretched arms.

"See you at the party," he said, mouthing the words broadly. He knew she could not hear above the racket. She waved back and smiled.

The words of the song flashed through Jonathan's brain: *I believe in you.* Oh, yeah, thought Jonathan. This Allison was a girl you could believe in.

The party after the concert was even wilder than the concert. The room was wall-to-wall with fans and friends and friends-of-friends. It seemed as though the tour sponsors had invited just about everybody they knew in New York. And anybody they didn't know had been invited by *Teen Rhythm* magazine.

Joe kept staring at an attractive young girl wearing a black T-shirt under a silk jacket. She had beautiful red hair, freckles, and a face-crinkling smile. When he asked her name, the girl seemed surprised.

"Joe McIntyre, don't you remember me?" she asked. "I'm Sara Flynn from Lebanon, Indiana. We met just this morning at the World Trade Center."

"Not the Girl Scouts!" Joe was flabbergasted.

"You don't think we go everywhere in those green uniforms, do you? The big guy, your bodyguard, Biscuit? He got us party invitations after we spent all that time posing with you."

"You sure look"—Joe searched for the right word—"*different!* What's that T-shirt? Heavy metal?"

"Yeah," the redheaded girl said. "I listen to all kinds of stuff, even classical music. But I have to be honest. I wasn't a *real* New Kids fan until tonight. You guys are *way* cool."

"Hey, I never was much into Girl

Scouts, either," said Joe. "This is really trippin'."

"We watched your elephant ride on the evening news in our hotel room," the girl said. "That must have been awesome!"

Joe took Sara over to the refreshment table. On the way they bumped into Danny, sipping on something in a tall paper cup.

"Biscuit got me some soybean juice." Danny smiled. "He knows how I hate this party junk food."

Joe smiled back as he led Sara toward the punch bowl. He made a rotating, that-guy-must-be-crazy sign with his index finger and nodded his head in Danny's direction. Danny didn't mind. He was used to all the jokes the other New Kids made about his healthy eating habits.

Danny craned his neck to see above the crowd, looking for Jordan and Jonathan. Tonight the two seemed to be back on track. Singing and dancing together had made them feel like brothers again, Danny guessed.

Then he saw Allison, the cause of all the trouble. She seemed to be looking for Jonathan, too. She was standing on tiptoe, looking all around the room. Danny noticed that Allison was wearing the old crumpled hat Jon had had on for the concert.

She caught Jonathan's eye, but he was at the far end of the room, talking with a bunch of record executive-types. Jonathan waved to her and gave a little shrug. He could not get away. Danny saw Allison smile and wave back, then turn toward the door.

"Good," Danny said to himself. "Allison's leaving. That means we won't have another Knight fight tonight." Danny let himself feel proud of his rhyme: "No Knight fight tonight—all *right!*" And he took a big sip of his cranberry-yogurt, vitamin-enriched soybean drink.

"Danny Wood!" called a voice behind him.

Danny turned to see a thin lady with thick blond hair coming toward him. She had narrow eyes and a broad mouth set into a sharp face. The way she walked, pushing her way through the crowd, told Danny right away that she was a bodybuilder.

"You're the New Kid I've been dying to

meet!" she bellowed. "You really put on a show tonight. I loved that handstand you did. Boy, you *really* put on a show tonight."

Danny gave a weak smile, considering his chances for escape. They were less than good.

"Say, is that a soybean malted you're drinking? I love that stuff, you know? I used to drink yogurt-culture malteds, you know? But they kind of leave a, you know, like, mustache-thing.

"So, do you, like, work out every day? Do you have your own weight room and your own Nautilus machines, or what?"

Danny had the sinking feeling that this woman was going to ask to feel his muscles. Or worse yet, ask him to feel hers. Just then, out of the corner of his eye, he saw something very curious.

Allison was coming back into the room. Only this time she was wearing Jordan's Mets cap instead of the old porkpie Jonathan had given her. Maybe Danny was wrong about a peaceful end to this difficult day.

"I probably weigh a lot more than you

think," said the bodybuilder woman. "So, how much do you think I weigh?"

She put her arm around his shoulder and pulled him aside. Danny lost sight of Allison. "Come on. What do you say? A hundred and twenty, a hundred and thirty?"

"Sure," Danny agreed, just to shut her up. "Maybe one twenty-five, huh?"

The woman gave a head-bobbing laugh that sounded like a snort. "One twenty-five! Not! How 'bout one sixty-eight?"

"Come on!" Danny really didn't care if she weighed a hundred pounds or three hundred.

"No bull," the woman insisted. "And every ounce muscle. Feel this."

She flexed her biceps, and what had seemed to be a skinny arm under a beaded sweatsuit sleeve suddenly bulged out. Danny obliged, giving her muscle the test.

"Solid," he agreed.

Danny could not bring himself to look around. He felt as though everyone in the place must be staring at him and laughing.

But as the woman went on and on, he

took a chance and glanced about the room. Surprisingly, the party was going on just as before. No one seemed to notice him and "Honey Hulk" here.

Even more surprising, Allison Holtz was coming his way, wearing not Jordan's baseball cap, but Jonathan's porkpie. Now, when did she change hats again? Danny wondered.

"I can't find Jonathan," she said, "to tell him how much I enjoyed the concert."

"Then tell *me*," Jordan said, coming up behind Danny. "What happened to my Mets cap?"

"Oh, Jordan, hi!" Allison said innocently. "Your cap? Oh, uh, I let my friend wear it for a while."

"Your friend?" Danny asked.

"Yeah, she . . . she came to the concert with me, and now she's waiting outside," Allison said. "She was really getting jealous, so I let her wear your cap."

"You ought to bring her in," said Danny. "I'd like to meet her."

"We've kinda got to get home," Allison said. She seemed to grow suddenly nervous. "My friend's parents don't like her staying out too late."

76

"Hi everybody," said the bodybuilder, just because no one was paying her any attention. "I'm Juanita. I do makeup."

"Hi, Juanita," said Jordan politely. He turned back to Allison. "So, will you be at the photo sessions tomorrow?"

"I'm not sure," said Allison. "That kind of depends on what Shaka wants me to do, I guess. Maybe."

"I also do bodybuilding." Juanita did her best to work her way into the conversation.

"Well, I'll talk to Shaka," said Jordan. He leaned over hoping to give Allison a kiss, but she was already heading off.

"And bring your sister," Danny called after her.

"You really do makeup?" Jordan asked the unusual Juanita.

"Oh, yeah. Low-budget movies, a few commercials, off-Broadway shows, some demos at the department stores in Jersey. And I work out a lot. Wanta feel my muscles? How much you think I weigh? Danny, don't tell him."

Danny and Jordan looked at each other. They were both wishing they had an excuse like Allison's. Sometimes they could get trapped for hours at one of these parties.

Jordan tried an old line. "Well, Danny, we got a long day ahead of us tomorrow. Better get to bed."

But Juanita the bodybuilding makeup artist wasn't going to be that easy to get rid of. "Maybe *you're* flakin' out, Jordan, but not Danny. If you ate the right stuff, like Danny here, you'd have more energy. Danny, you got any more of that soybean drink for Jordan?"

Sometimes they could get trapped for *hours* at one of these parties.

Chapter

6

ALLISON HOLTZ SAT at the old dressing table that had been her grandmother's. In the mirror she could see the two hats hanging on the wall of the room she shared with her sister.

She looked at the bright blue baseball cap with the orange *M* and the battered old black felt hat. Whatever happened, those two hats would always be on the wall, reminding her of this unbelievable day.

The house was quiet. The streets of Brooklyn were silent, except for a distant siren and a train whistle that seemed even farther off. It was nearly two in the morning, and she was wide awake.

Allison brushed her long, soft brown hair and looked at herself in the mirror. The dark eyes seemed full of questions as they stared back at her. She heard her sister, Stacey, finishing up brushing her teeth in the bathroom.

Thank goodness for Stacey, Allison thought. There are times in your life when the only one you can turn to is a sister. I wonder if it's the same way with brothers. Do Jonathan and Jordan depend on each other the way Stacey and I do?

After a moment Stacey came into the bedroom, wearing a peach nightgown that, except for its color, was just the same as Allison's pale blue one. Most of their clothes were just alike.

Stacey stopped and took the baseball cap from the wall. "Maybe I'll sleep in it," she said. She picked up the program from the concert and a one-page advertisement for a New Kids album fell out onto the floor. Stacey picked up the sheet and quickly turned it into a paper airplane. With a perfect aim, she flew the airplane into the back of Allison's head.

"Ouch!"

"Just wanted to see if I could still do that," said Stacey. "One of the few important trade secrets revealed to me by our dear father."

Allison smiled as Stacey came over to the edge of the bed and sat down next to her. The two pairs of big brown eyes looked at each other in the dressing table mirror. Instead of questions, now Allison saw laughter in these eyes.

There was absolutely no difference between Stacey's eyes and Allison's. There was no difference in their hair, either. In fact, the two faces in the mirror looked exactly alike. Allison and Stacey were identical twins.

Pulling on the baseball cap, Stacey said, "You know, Alli, there have been times when I wanted to choke you. But days like today make it all okay, you know?"

"Make *what* okay, Stace?" asked Allison, pretending she didn't already know the answer.

"Being identical twins, you ditz." Stacey slapped her playfully with the Mets cap.

"There were times *today* when I

wanted to choke you, Stace," Allison retorted.

"Hey, I filled in for you just like you wanted," Stacey said. "Unless I'm mistaken, *you* were the one who didn't show up at the ferry terminal."

"And *you* were the one who walked off and left, before I got there," Allison complained. "I could have lost my job!"

"Hey, girl, the boat was leaving! Besides, I had to go get ready for the concert. You don't want me to go out smelling like Bimbo the Elephant Girl, do you? Besides, you were out finding another job."

"Oh, yeah, I guess so," said Allison. "But you know, I can't just quit something like *Teen Rhythm* because I get one little part in one off-Broadway show. Who knows if it's gonna work?"

Stacey laid back on the bed, twirling her Mets cap on a finger. She had reluctantly agreed to fill in for Allison at her *Teen Rhythm* job while Allison ran off to audition for a part in a play.

In a way, Stacey thought, I was the actress today, pretending to be Allison, riding through the streets on an elephant, holding tight to Jordan, having lunch with the New Kids on the Block.

But pretending to be Allison was probably the only acting role Stacey would ever play. Allison had the true dramatic talent in the Holtz family. Stacey knew her role would be that of a nurse, and she was happy about that.

"It's gonna work, Alli. Your agent said this is the part for you, didn't he? You've had your lines memorized for weeks, just in case you *did* get the job.

"So now you've got the job. And besides, you've got what it takes. You're gonna be famous, and then I can be your agent."

"You may have to be my nurse when Daddy finds out. You know how he feels about the theater."

"'Get a real job, Allison. Go into medicine, like your sister. Those show business people are no good.'" She imitated her father's familiar words. "I'm supposed to start in that play tomorrow, and I haven't even *told* Dad about it yet."

"You've got to tell him, Alli. No way are you gonna start going out at night and leave me to cover for you."

"I don't know what to do, Stace. Even if he doesn't put me in the hospital, he'll probably kick me out. Then I might need two jobs just to pay my room and board."

Stacey threw herself back on the bed and groaned. "You've been watching soap operas again. Daddy's not like that, Alli. He's not gonna kick you out. Get real. And, look, if he thinks show business people are bad news, just introduce him to the New Kids."

Allison plopped down on the bed next to her sister. Not a bad idea, she thought, although Allison doubted she could ever pull it off. She took the baseball cap from Stacey and put it over her face.

"Kinda reminds me of Jordan Knight," she said. "You like that guy, don't you?"

"Only to die for," Stacey answered. Unable to control herself, she closed her eyes and squealed, *"Aaaaa! Jordan!"*

Allison quickly grabbed a pillow and covered her sister's mouth to stifle the scream. "Quiet, you dweeb! You'll wake up the whole house."

"Jordan!" Stacey sighed, softly this time. "Mmmm. Like, you don't feel the same way about Jonathan, I suppose?"

"Jonathan!" Mocking her sister's hysteria, Allison pulled the pillow over her own face to muffle the squeal: *"Aaaaaa!"*

Stacey laughed. "Once again twins will be twins. Hey, it could be worse, Alli. We could be in love with the same brother."

Suddenly Allison sat up. "Uh-oh. Wait a minute, Stace. You're right, that would be a real bummer."

"Only we're not. So?"

"So, that's the fix we put them in, Jonathan and Jordan. They *think* they like the same sister: me."

"Allison, you're right. I felt it when I was in the bus with them this afternoon. Jonathan was doing anything he could think of to take my attention away from Jordan. And I think the other guys were picking up on it, too.

"The vibes in that bus were bad. Jordan and Jonathan are *competing* with each other over what they think is the same girl."

"Only we're not."

"Only we're not," Stacey agreed. "So how do we let them in on that little secret? They might not like being tricked."

"That, my dear twin-chickie, is going to take both our little brains to figure out."

"Okay," said Stacey, "but tomorrow."

"Agreed," said Allison, taking down the porkpie hat and hugging it to her chest.

Soon they were both asleep.

Chapter

7

THE NEXT MORNING Stacey was doing her hair when the phone rang. Allison had already gone, so Stacey went to answer it. But when the ringing suddenly stopped, she knew her father had gotten there first. Letting him answer the phone turned out to be a big mistake.

"Stacey, come down here!" he shouted from the living room.

She came down the stairs, wondering what the problem could be. She knew as soon as she heard her father say, "That was Allison's *agent* on the phone."

Mr. Holtz was normally a gentle man.

Tall, muscular, and soft-spoken, he had raised his two daughters since his wife died. That had been nearly twelve years ago. He was determined that his girls "make something of themselves." But being in *show business,* as he called it, was not what Mr. Holtz had in mind.

"I thought your sister had given up this show business stuff," he said.

"But, Daddy, everybody else keeps telling her to go for it. She's got what it takes to be an actress."

"No, she doesn't," said her father angrily. "Because one thing it takes is my permission, and she doesn't have that."

"What did the agent have to say?" Stacey asked innocently.

"He said I should be proud of her. He said she 'knocked 'em dead' at her audition—whatever that means. And he said they want her at the theater this afternoon for costume and makeup.

"I'll tell you what *I* want, Stacey. I want you to go find your sister and tell her to stay with that magazine job, where she can learn something useful. She could be anything she wants there—a receptionist, even a secretary. Allison's got a good head on her shoulders."

Stacey nodded and kept her mouth shut. Mr. Holtz loved his daughters and cared about them, but he didn't really understand them.

A telephone call to the *Teen Rhythm* office told Stacey what she needed to know. She had to catch up with Allison to make sure she showed up at the theater on time. This could be her sister's big break. Her best chance for finding Allison and the New Kids would be at the Bronx Zoo. They were due there in just about an hour.

Stacey tried to remember exactly how Allison had dressed that morning. She might be called upon to step in for her twin again.

My big chance to be an actress, Stacey thought. It's the only part I'll ever play, the role of my own twin sister. Too bad I'll never be able to take a bow.

For the New Kids it was a fast-paced, crazy morning.

They started out with a ride through Central Park in the horse-drawn carriages. Allison drove Monica Merriweather's battered orange Volkswagen Beetle so that Monica could jump out along the way to take pictures. And there were lots of pictures to take. The concert's success and last night's party had left the boys in a mood for clowning around. They didn't seem tired at all.

Donnie traded jackets and hats with the carriage driver. He sat up front on the driver's seat while the driver pretended to be one of the New Kids. Since the driver was a heavy black woman, the *Teen Rhythm* readers were not going to be fooled by the photographs.

As the carriage rolled past a lake filled with toy sailboats, Joe hung by his knees from the back of the carriage. The others pretended they were trying to dump him off. Monica took several shots of that.

They got off to climb around a bronze statue of Alice in Wonderland. Donnie, still wearing the carriage driver's outfit, struck a comical pose with the Mad Hatter.

Nearing the end of the ride they caught up with a team of bicycle riders who pleaded for New Kids' autographs. Monica stood up in her car and stuck her head through the sunroof to take pictures. The boys signed the backs of the cyclists' shirts.

Soon the carriage pulled to a stop near the Plaza Hotel, where Shaka Tosulu was waiting for them. It was Joe who spotted a big children's toy store across Fifth Avenue.

"Toys!" shouted Joe. "Let's go."

"Wait!" called Shaka. "Our schedule says . . ."

But it was too late. The traffic signal said Walk, but Donnie, Danny, Jordan, and Jonathan were running to catch up with the youngest member of the New Kids.

Shaka shrugged. "You might as well bring your cameras, Monica. I'll try to make peace with the store managers. Allison, don't let them go wild."

But Allison was the wrong person to calm down the New Kids, especially Jonathan and Jordan Knight. Inside the store the two brothers tried to outdo each other, showing off for Allison.

"Hey, Allison, dig this electric Lamborghini," called Jonathan. He was sitting scrunched up behind the steering wheel of a working toy sports car.

"Yo, Allison!" Jordan shouted. "Check out this space shuttle!"

A scale model of the space shuttle *Co-*

lumbia came gliding through the air. It nearly took down a display of Lego toys and just missed the expensive hairdo of a shopping grandmother. Allison threw her hands up to cover her face when Danny gave one of his balletlike leaps to catch the shuttle in midair.

The Knight brothers charged into the stuffed animal department, each determined to buy something very expensive for Allison. They went through the toys like a double tornado, picking up one animal after another and handing it to Allison. The constant flash of Monica's camera and the laughter of shoppers only made matters worse.

Determined not to let them buy anything for her, Allison accepted each toy, admired it, then put it back in its place.

Teddy bears, koalas, furry cats, and sad-faced hound dogs: Allison admired them all, then returned them to their displays. Jonathan led her to a giant panda, which would never fit into her room. She just smiled and shook her head.

"I don't need any stuffed animals," she said. "Really, I don't even *like* stuffed animals!"

Then Jordan's hand popped up over the

back of a huge giraffe. It was holding a life-size toy sharpei.

"Nikko!" Allison cried. "It's adorable!"

She held the lifelike toy and rubbed the wrinkles on its head. It felt just like the New Kids mascot. She couldn't bear to put it back.

"Okay, Jordan," she said. "Thank you for a very special present."

Monica snapped a photo of Jordan pretending to chase Donnie with the imitation dog. As Jordan was paying for "Nikko" at the cash register, Shaka clapped her long, ebony hands together and said:

"Attention, please! New Kids bus departing for Bronx Zoo in one minute. All aboard right now!"

As they boarded the bus, Danny watched Allison playfully nuzzle Jonathan's ear with the stuffed sharpei. But Jonathan ignored her. Uh-oh, thought Danny, he's sulking again. He can't stand that Allison accepted that present from Jordan. Here we go again.

When they arrived at the entrance to the zoo, Jonathan excused himself, saying he would catch up with the gang in a few minutes. Shaka handed out copies of a zoo brochure to everyone present, including Monica and Allison. She had circled all the exhibits they would be visiting.

Jonathan didn't even look at the brochure. Instead, he watched the gang walk away. Allison was still carrying the toy dog Jordan had bought her. Jonathan did not feel like doing any more sightseeing, and he'd had just about enough picture-taking for one trip.

Jonathan walked over to a concession stand and got himself a soda. At first he considered getting a bag of popcorn, too, but he changed his mind. He didn't feel much like eating, either. He was just looking forward to doing their second and final Madison Square Garden concert on Saturday night and leaving New York City. Jonathan couldn't remember what the next city on the tour was supposed to be. Wherever they were going, Allison wouldn't be there.

Suddenly Allison *was* there, standing right in front of him, looking kind of lost. She must have felt bad about the way she'd been treating him!

"Yo, Allison," he called out. "How 'bout some popcorn and a soda?" Jonathan had no way of knowing that he was talking to Stacey, Allison's identical twin sister.

Stacey was surprised to see Jonathan. She had hoped to be able to attract her sister's attention and speak to her without being seen by the New Kids. Instead, she would have to pretend again.

Don't panic, she told herself. Just think of how Allison would handle this situation. She certainly did not want to do anything that would damage her sister's friendship with Jonathan.

"What are you doing here all by yourself?" Stacey asked.

"I can't take any more kidding around, Allison. I just had to be by myself for a while."

"That's cool. Uh, where do you think the others are, right about now?"

"You should know," Jonathan replied. "I mean, you just left them, right?"

"Sure. Right. I just meant, do you think they're having fun?" Stacey chose her words carefully.

"I guess. Seems like you and Jordan have a great time together any time you're around animals. Like, the circus elephant ride, then the stuffed animals.

"Hey, wait a minute," Jonathan interrupted himself. "Where's Nikko?"

Stacey didn't know what Jonathan was talking about. Surely the New Kids would not take their pet into the zoo. What if he jumped into the lions' cage? Maybe Allison had taken Nikko for a walk before she went in. That must be it.

"Nikko's back on the bus," she said, hoping she was correct.

That must have been the right thing to say, because it brought a smile to Jonathan's face. He bought another soda and a box of popcorn.

"How about a ride on that monorail?" Jonathan suggested. He pointed to the sky lift that carried visitors from one end of the huge lift to the other.

"Sure," said Stacey. At least on the monorail they would not be bumping into Allison.

"Chillin'! I've got a thing or two I'd like to say to you, girl." Jonathan put his arm around Stacey's shoulder and walked toward the sky lift entrance.

Oh, great! thought Stacey. Now I'd

better be really friendly to Jonathan or he'll think Allison doesn't like him. Good move, Stacey.

As the monorail lifted off, Stacey half-listened to Jonathan. He was blabbering on about the tough life the New Kids led. They never stayed in one place long enough to develop lasting relationships. Girls were always after them, but never really got to *know* them. Allison was different . . . and so on.

Stacey wasn't listening. She was too busy trying to figure out a way out of this mess. She just *had* to tell Allison about her agent's call and the way their father had reacted.

Absentmindedly, Stacey stared down at the folded-up Bronx Zoo brochure that Jonathan was still holding. She could see that some of the exhibits were circled in blue ink, with numbers written next to them. She leaned closer to the brochure as Jonathan chattered on to get a better look. The big cats were number one, followed by the bird exhibit, then the World of Darkness.

The World of Darkness! That gave Stacey an idea. She looked down and saw they were coming to the lions and tigers. There were the New Kids, posing with a balloon vendor on the ground below. She saw Allison, standing behind the camera elf, waving her arms at the boys. In the seat beside her, Jonathan was looking off into the distance.

Quickly Stacey pulled a lipstick from her purse. With it she drew a big red star around the World of Darkness. Then she scribbled "Meet me. Stace."

She folded the brochure into a sleek paper airplane, just the way her father had taught her. She sailed the paper airplane right at her sister, just as the monorail passed overhead. Thank goodness Jonathan was still occupied by his own story and watching the animals on the other side.

Looking back, she saw the airplane slide to a stop at Allison's feet. Allison started to bend down to pick it up, but the monorail turned a curve and Stacey could not be sure she got the message. She would just have to take the chance.

"You know what I'd like to see, Jon?" she asked.

Jonathan gave her a puzzled look, as though wondering whether she'd been listening to any of his speech. Of course, she hadn't.

"I'd like to see that nocturnal exhibit."

"Huh?"

"You know, like, all those animals that come alive at night," Stacey explained.

"Oh, you mean like the New Kids on the Block?" Jonathan gave one of his famous laughs. *Hawr-hawr-hawr.*

"I don't think so," said Stacey with a smile. "I meant the World of Darkness."

"Okay," said Jonathan, baring his teeth and holding up his hands like claws. "But vatch out for vampire bats. *Hawr-hawr-hawr!*"

There really *were* vampire bats in the World of Darkness exhibit. There were opossums and big-eyed monkeys, strange lizards, and slinking cats. All these animals were in special enclosures, behind wires or glass. They were dimly lit by eerie blue lights, while the human visitors stood in total darkness to watch them.

Stacey, still pretending to be Allison, kept Jonathan as long as she could at each exhibit. She asked him every question she could think up about each animal. She wanted to keep Jonathan there until Allison arrived at the World of Darkness.

"Oh, look at that frog!" whispered Stacey. "He's got almost as many wrinkles as Nikko."

She bent down close to see the fat, bug-eyed frog. It was sitting on a half-submerged log in a swamp exhibit. Just as she brought her face level with the frog's, the creature puffed itself up and gave out an enormous *Crooooak!*

Stacey jumped backward with a little shriek, and Jonathan said, "Sounds like Jordan's latest love song. *Hawr-hawr-hawr!*"

"Not funny, Jon," said Stacey, thinking of how sweet Jordan had sounded when he sang "I Believe in You" to her at the concert last night.

"No, you're right," Jonathan said, bending down for a closer look at the funny-faced frog. "That's how Jordan sounds after he eats a pepperoni and olive pizza with double cheese. *Hawr-hawr-hawr! Hawr-hawr-hawr!*"

As Jonathan laughed, he felt a twinge of guilt. Making jokes about his brother was one thing, but he was beginning to enjoy it too much. What was happening?

Stacey felt someone's hand on her shoulder and heard a whisper in her ear. "Stace," the voice said, "it's Alli."

Allison pulled her sister away from the swamp exhibit as Jonathan straightened up. "This must be a frog from the banks of the River Jordan!" he said. *"Hawr-hawr-hawr!"*

"I heard that laugh the minute we walked in," Allison said. "The other guys will be here any second. I got your note."

"We've gotta get out of here without them seeing me," Stacey whispered. "You take over with Jonathan, and I'll wait for you by the zoo entrance."

"What's the matter?" Allison asked.

"Plenty," Stacey said. "Get away as soon as you can."

At that moment they heard Jordan's voice calling. "Allison? Is that you, Allison?"

"Be nice to my Jordan," Stacey whispered, hurrying off toward the exit.

Allison held out her left hand and felt someone take it. She thought it was Jordan, but in the dark she couldn't be sure.

Then someone took her right hand, the one holding her toy Nikko.

"There you are," said Jordan.

"There you are," said Jonathan. Then, feeling the stuffed sharpei, he added, "Hey, I thought you left this animal on the bus."

"Oh, no," said Jordan, "it's Jonathan. I thought we left *that* animal on the bus."

"All right, you guys," said Allison, pulling away from both of them. "That's enough! I'm not going to stay here and let you keep arguing over me."

"But, Allison—" Jonathan began.

"You've gotta decide which one of us you like," said Jordan.

"Right," said Jonathan, "and the other one will just have to back off."

"Okay," said Allison. "I'll decide. I'll meet you tonight. I'll take you all to a play, and when it's over, one of you can take me to dinner. Okay?"

"Cool," said Jordan and Jonathan together. In the darkness they could not see the determined looks on each other's faces.

"I'll meet you tonight in Greenwich Village," said Allison. "Seven o'clock at

Washington Square Park. And bring Danny and Joe and Donnie, too. I want all the New Kids *together* on this."

Allison turned into the darkness and was gone. The Knight brothers did not feel very together at that moment.

Chapter

8

THE NEW KIDS and their *Teen Rhythm* friends enjoyed lunch in Little Italy, one of New York City's most famous ethnic neighborhoods. This gave Shaka another chance to talk about the way so many different kinds of people could get along together in one place.

"Here, in the space of a few square blocks," she said, "you will find people from Rome and Naples and Milan. You will find families from Sardinia and from Sicily.

"And when you cross Canal Street, what do you find then?" she asked.

Donnie was slurping up a fork-full of

linguine and clam sauce, but he tried to answer. "Canals must mean Venice, huh? That's in Italy too, right?"

"True enough," said Shaka, "but in New York, crossing Canal Street means crossing from Italy into China. That's where we find Chinatown! We'll take a few photographs there after lunch, and that will wind up this assignment for us."

"You mean we'll have a day in New York without Monica and her cameras?" Joe asked.

"I'll bet you'll be glad to see the end of me," Monica said. She popped a flash in Joe's face as he sprinkled cheese on his ravioli and meat sauce.

"Nah," said Joe. "You oughta come with us. I'm just learning how to say *Gorgonzola* every time I do something cute. Say, Mon, is this cheese Gorgonzola?"

"Parmesan and Romano, most likely," she said, swinging around to face Danny. "Say *Romano,* Danny."

"Romano," Danny said, holding up a long, rubbery tentacle. He stuck out his tongue to pull it in his mouth as Monica's flash went off. "Mmmm," said Danny. "Scungili!"

"Gross," said Joe.

"What *is* that stuff?" Jonathan asked.

"You don't want to know," said Jordan.

"Man, I want to know everything," said Jonathan. "Some people enjoy their ignorance, but I gotta *know*, you know?"

Jordan looked at his brother and shook his head with disgust.

"Hey, what's that supposed to mean?" Jonathan asked, in an angry tone.

"Would you guys cool it?" Danny broke in. Trying to change the subject, he asked Shaka whether they should take a supply of New Kids shirts and caps with them to Chinatown.

"That might be a good idea," Shaka said. "We could give some away to the kids, and they would pose with you. That would be nice. I think they are having some sort of celebration there today, and there will be big crowds in those narrow streets."

Donnie was finished with his meal, so he offered to go to the bus and get a supply of shirts and caps.

Danny could still feel the tension in the air between the Knight brothers. He wondered whether bringing the problem out in the open would help things or just make them worse. He decided to try it.

"Look, guys," he said to Jordan and Jonathan, "we're going to be leaving New York after the concert tomorrow night. Do you think you can solve this Allison problem by then?"

"We've got no problem," Jordan said. "Allison's gonna take care of everything tonight when she says, 'Jordan, you're the one.' All will be most cool, Danny Boy."

"You'll be cool, all right," Jonathan said. "Because I'm hot. For once, Jordan, we've found a girl who's got brains enough to see through your Mister Cool act."

Danny tried to stop the argument by saying that dessert was on the way, but the brothers kept it up.

"Maybe you didn't see the way Allison lit up when I sang to her the other night," Jordan said.

"Right, Jordan," Jonathan exploded. "You can sing to the girls, but you never learned how to talk to them. Those dumb rhymes of yours don't make it in conversation. Like:

107

"Hello, miss, we are big stars,
My name's Jordan, what is yours?
Hawr-hawr-hawr!"

The waiter was just setting down a dessert plate in front of Jordan. Without stopping to think, Jordan scooped up a cannoli—a fat roll of pastry stuffed with sweet cream and covered with powdered sugar. He slammed it into the front of Jonathan's shirt. The dessert went flying all over the place, even on Jonathan's face.

"Laugh at *that!*" Jordan said with a mean grin as he got up from the table.

Everyone else was stunned. Jonathan looked as though he had lost a pie-throwing contest. Joe tried to stifle a laugh, but milk came bubbling up at the corners of his mouth.

"Okay, Jordan, that's it." Jonathan stood up angrily, wiping his face and shirt with a red-and-white napkin. "You're about to get what's been coming to you for a long time."

"You're just so *sweet* with that powdered sugar in your hair. Makes you look your age." Jordan pushed back his chair and sneered at his brother. Everyone in the little restaurant was pointing and staring.

Jordan imitated Jonathan's laugh. Jonathan lunged across the table at him, but Jordan was too fast. He was out the door and into the street, still laughing as Jonathan took after him.

"No pictures," Jonathan said to Monica Merriweather on his way out. "I'm gonna kill that little sucker."

"No!" shouted Shaka. "Brothers are not supposed to act this way. Please come back!"

But it was too late. Jonathan took off after his brother, chasing him down the street. Danny decided it was time for him to take over.

"Shaka," Danny said, "you and Monica get back to the bus. Keep the bodyguards occupied, but don't tell them what happened, please. We can't let Dick Scott find out about this!"

At that moment Donnie stepped into the restaurant with a shopping bag full of New Kids souvenirs. "What's going on?" he wondered.

"Posse up!" Danny shouted. "We've gotta stop those crazy Knight brothers before they get us all in deep trouble."

With Donnie Wahlberg and Joe McIntyre in tow, Danny Wood took off through the streets of Little Italy. Flags of red, white, and green flew past in a blur. Danny's high-tops slapped the pavement in a rhythm that sounded like a drum track from their new album.

Almost without warning, the colors of Little Italy changed to the gold and red-orange of Chinatown. Streets that had been blocked off to traffic were clogged instead with pedestrians. Many in the crowd were Oriental-Americans dressed in the elaborate costumes of their ancestral country.

Jordan disappeared into the crowd. Jonathan pulled up at a corner and looked for his brother. He was not sure which way he had gone.

Jonathan hoisted himself up onto a short wall of concrete that stuck out from the entrance to a basement newsstand. The wall was pasted over with posters, newspapers, and advertisements. None of them had English-style lettering but instead were covered with Chinese words that were strange to Jonathan's eye. Inside the newsstand door he could see a rack of music tapes, but he could not recognize a single name or title. He guessed there was not one New Kids tape in the bunch.

To keep his balance, Jonathan leaned against the plate-glass window of a grocery store. The words *Hong Fat Provisions* were painted on the glass. Inside, a row of what looked like smoked ducks hung by their necks to dry. The ducks were missing only their feathers.

Turning to the sea of foreign faces in the street, Jonathan searched for a sign of Jordan. Behind him came a tapping on the glass. He looked to see a round-faced little man with large ears, frowning through the ducks. The man was shaking his head and wagging a finger at Jonathan. Although Jonathan couldn't understand the man's language, he knew what the grocer was saying:

"Get off my window. Go away, boy."

Jonathan felt like a stranger in a strange land. In Chinatown he was just another tourist. He wondered whether anyone here had even heard of the New Kids on the Block.

Then he heard familiar squeals coming from the next corner.

"New Kids! New Kids!"

"Jordan!"

"Eeeeee!"

A crowd of girls was pouring out a building that might have been a school. They had Jordan trapped. The girls were sweeping him around a corner, like a human flood carrying a log. The girls were pulling at his clothes and hair.

All at once, a familiar feeling came over Jonathan. It was the old, protective concern he felt for all his New Kids buddies, but especially for his younger brother. That concern had been there all along, he knew, but it was hidden for the past two days by his feelings for Allison and by the jealousy those feelings had created.

Someone was tugging at Jonathan's sleeve. For an instant he thought he was about to share Jordan's fate. But instead of screaming fans, it was the angry old grocer, fussing in Chinese.

He smiled at the almond-eyed little man and flashed him a peace sign. Then he hopped down to the sidewalk, hearing Donnie's voice:

"Yo, Jon! You okay?"

"I'm cool," Jonathan replied, "but Jordan's got girl trouble."

Joe and Danny joined Donnie and Jonathan. "Still fighting over Allison, you mean?" asked Joe.

"No, no," Jonathan protested. "I'm talking about fan trouble. They've got Jordan surrounded up ahead, and he needs help big time."

With Jonathan in the lead, the New Kids pushed through the crowd. They heard popping sounds and children's screams. It was not gunshots but firecrackers exploding. Suddenly, from all sides, people were throwing bundles of small firecrackers on the ground. They went off one after another in a string of crackling explosions. The boys had wandered right into the middle of a Chinese celebration.

Just ahead Jordan was shut up tight in a red telephone booth. The booth was crowned with an elaborate carved roof in the shape of a Chinese pagoda. The fans had Jordan surrounded and were rocking the phone booth back and forth as they chanted his name.

"Jor-dan! Jor-dan!"

Jordan stared out, wide-eyed, with a look somewhere between a grin and panic.

113

"Somebody's going to get hurt," Danny said, "and it might be Jordan."

"Hold it!" Jonathan blurted out. "I've got an idea. Look at those guys."

Around a street corner a group of Chinese boys were stretching out a long silk sheet. It was green and red and gold and painted to look like the long body of a dragon.

"That's a dragon puppet," Jon explained.

One of the boys lifted up a huge, flame-breathing dragon head made of silk and paper. He began to put it over his own head and mount it on his shoulders, but Jonathan rushed over to stop him.

"You speak English?" he asked the boys.

"Sure, man," one of them wisecracked. "Do you?"

"We need help," Jonathan said, explaining Jordan's problem.

Donnie pulled out New Kids T-shirts and hats from his shopping bag and passed them out to the dragon crew. Delighted with their gifts, the boys agreed to lend their dragon for a few minutes.

Jonathan put on the dragon's head.

The other New Kids lined up behind him, covering themselves with the green silk "body" of the creature. As soon as they were all in place, Jonathan started a shuffling dance step toward the pagoda phone booth. To keep the others in rhythm, Jon hummed the rocking intro to "The Right Stuff."

> *"Oh-uh-oh a-oh-oh*
> *Oh-uh-oh-a-oh*
> *The Right Stuff!"*

The dragon began its wobbly, wiggling movement and the people in the crowd gathered around. They were surprised to hear the dragon singing.

Children began to throw firecrackers at the dragon's feet. This was part of the tradition, to make the dragon "dance." Danny hopped around like crazy, trying to keep the firecrackers from ruining his new high-tops.

Jonathan, peeping out through the dragon's mouth, could see the phone booth getting closer. He lowered the big head and pushed into the crowd of girls.

"Eeee!" they screamed. "Dragon is here! Look out!"

The ocean of girls parted, and Jonathan saw his way clear to the phone booth. A few shuffling steps more, and he was at the door.

"Grab him, guys!" Jonathan shouted back over his shoulder.

At the tail of the dragon Joe and Donnie lifted up the silk sheet. They saw Jordan's face fill with surprise and delight as he recognized his buddies. Joe pushed open the phone booth door and pulled Jordan into the dragon.

"Just hang on to Donnie and start dancin'," he said, laughing. "Your brother's leading the act."

Joe could not see Jordan's smile, but he heard it in his voice. "Right now," Jordan said, "I'd follow that brother of mine *anywhere*."

Chapter

9

GREENWICH VILLAGE had been a favorite spot for artists, writers, musicians, and other show business types for years and years, so the New Kids on the Block felt right at home there. On a Friday night people were out everywhere.

The boys left the bus on one of the Village's tree-lined streets, where brownstone apartment stairs ended right at the sidewalk. As they began walking, Jonathan noticed that the water stain had disappeared completely from Jordan's favorite leather jacket.

Jonathan said he was glad the jacket

hadn't been damaged, and Jordan seemed pleased by Jon's show of concern. On such a cool night the jacket would come in handy, Jonathan added.

Danny listened to their conversation and smiled to himself. He was just happy the two brothers were back on the same team. Now, if Allison could just manage not to set them off again.

In the mood for a good time the New Kids made their way to Washington Square Park, the heart of the Village. They had some time to fool around before meeting Allison under the park's famous arch.

"Listen to the music," Donnie said as they approached the open space. There seemed to be all kinds of crazy sounds, bouncing off the walls of all the buildings around them.

"It sounds a lot like our band warming up," said Joe. "You can hear everybody doing something different, all at the same time."

When they stepped into the square, the boys understood the reason for the jumbled-up music. Four different groups were performing on the park's four corners. No group seemed to be aware of anything going on around them. They were all just happy to be making music in the chilly night air. This was just the way things happened in New York City.

"Let's go check them out," said Joe. He jumped into the lead and started an arm-swinging dance maneuver in the direction of the nearest musical group.

They came to a string quartet playing a classical piece. The sheet music was clipped to their music stands with clothespins to keep the cold wind from blowing it away.

The boys listened for a while and Jordan recognized the music as a quartet by a German composer named Franz Schubert.

"I can't remember the name of the piece," Jordan said, "but I think it has something to do with a fish."

Danny did some imitation ballet steps, leaping and twirling and making swimming motions with his arms. He said that had something to do with a fish, too.

The music ended with a loud buildup and all the bows rubbing across their strings like crazy. When the piece was over, the New Kids all joined a small crowd in applauding.

"That was pretty cool," Donnie had to admit. Joseph asked the musicians where they were from.

"The Juilliard School here in New York," answered a pretty blond girl, looking up from her cello. "All except Roger here. He's from the High School of the Performing Arts." She was pointing with her bow to a small young man.

Donnie noticed people dropping coins and dollar bills into a top hat on the sidewalk. "Do you guys earn a lot of money this way?" he asked.

"Not really," said Roger, the young string bass player. "But we get enough for pizza, and it's a great way to practice."

The boys thanked them for the music and walked to the next corner, where two old men sat on wooden crates playing guitar and harmonica. The older of the men wore dark glasses and looked as though he might be blind. Around his neck was a wire frame, which held a battered old tin harmonica.

"Listen to that old dude wail," said

Jonathan. "He's been singing the blues for a *long* time."

The other man picked up after the harmonica solo with lyrics about "muddy water risin'."

Again, the boys joined in the applause at the end of the tune. Again, there was a hat on the ground for contributions. This time it was a battered old straw hat, the kind a farmhand might wear.

"I bet one of those old guys used to pick cotton in this hat," Donnie said, dropping in some folded bills. He knew that the music he had just heard was part of history.

At the next corner, near the arch, the New Kids looked on in amazement at what they found. Three talented young men from the Caribbean islands were jamming, making beautiful music on a collection of old black oil drums. These homemade instruments sounded like giant xylophones.

The top of each steel drum was carefully hammered out to create a set of rounded domes. Each dome looked like an overturned bowl. Each bowl represented a note of the musical scale, and the name of the note was painted on the bowl in yellow.

The musicians could play almost anything just by hitting the bowls with hammers. They played folk music, then classical, then jazz and rock. Every number drew loud applause from the listeners.

This time there was a young woman in an island costume who passed through the audience with a tambourine. People dropped money into it to show their appreciation of the musicians' work.

"Yo! That's the original *heavy metal* band, huh?" Jordan joked.

"*Hawr-hawr-hawr!*" laughed Jonathan. "Imagine how those guys would sound with some high-powered amps!"

The last musician in the square was a small boy, all alone. He was using a pair of battered drumsticks on a strange assortment of metal pots and lids and plastic containers. He'd even put together a kind of cymbal tree, made of tin-can tops mounted on wire coat hangers.

"Look at that little guy go!" Joe exclaimed.

The New Kids looked on in astonishment as the boy's hands flew around his homemade drum set. He battered out complex rhythms that he seemed to make up as he went along. There seemed to be music playing in his head.

Unlike the other entertainers, the boy had no crowd gathered around him. The few onlookers who were there did not seem like the types to have much money in their pockets. The boy had a tin can on the ground in place of a hat, and it contained only a small bit of change.

Clearly, the young drummer came from a poor part of town. His clothes were tattered, and in spite of the cold, he wore a torn undershirt with no jacket or sweater. In spite of all this, the little boy played fiercely, as if his fingers were on fire.

"This guy is really smokin'," Danny said.

"The dude can drum," Joe agreed, "even on these plastic traps. But nobody's paying attention to him."

It was Donnie who had the idea: "The kid's problem is that he's stuck over here all by himself. He needs a bigger group to jam with. Let's help him out, huh?"

The New Kids took Donnie's lead. They fanned out around the square to convince the other musicians to join together for a jam session. Soon the other musicians—and their listeners—were trooping over to where the boy was playing. The little boy just kept on drumming, pretending not to notice the gathering crowd of people.

The other musicians arranged themselves around the little boy, just like an orchestra. The violinist, violist, cellist, and bass player; the blues guitarist and his harmonica man; the steel drummers —they were all ready to jam.

"All right," Jonathan called out. "We're the New Kids on the Block, and what we wanta hear is a song called 'Games.' Are you with me?"

Clapping out the rhythm and humming the tune, Donnie got everyone into the spirit of the song from the New Kids' *Step By Step* album:

> *"Somebody said somebody wouldn't last too long.*
> *Somebody keeps going strong.*

Roger, the young man from the Performing Arts high school, threw his bow on the ground and started slapping out the rhythm on his huge bass fiddle. The crowd cheered when he started spinning his fiddle, even though it was a lot bigger than he was.

The other stringed instruments formed a smooth background of shifting chords. There were just three of them, but in the park they sounded like the whole string section of an orchestra.

The old blues guitarist joined in, and the steel drummers became involved as well. As for the kid on the pots and cans, he pounded away, more frantic than before.

Meanwhile, the New Kids twirled and leapt as though the sidewalk of Washington Square was the stage at Madison Square Garden. Minute by minute, the crowd kept on growing, drawn by the greatest performance Washington Square Park had witnessed in a long, long time.

Standing on a bench nearby, Mr. Holtz watched with great interest. So these were the young men his daughter Allison wanted him to meet. There was no question that they had talent and energy. They also seemed to have a whole lot of heart.

"You're right," he said to the pretty girl at his side. "These guys are good. And you

125

can see they really *do* care about people. Look at how they're helping that little drummer boy."

Mr. Holtz could not stop his feet from tapping to the rhythm of the New Kids on the Block. "You know, Allison," he said, "we should go put some money in that can, too."

Mr. Holtz's daughter smiled. But it was not Allison. This was Stacey, pretending to be her sister!

The twins had not fooled their father since they were in fourth grade. That time resulted in stern words and a punishment. This time, though, Stacey figured it was all for a good cause. Still, she hated to trick her father like this. She sure hoped Allison knew what she was doing.

"You know, Dad," Stacey said, "those aren't just a bunch of street musicians out there. The string players are from some of the best music schools in the country. I've seen those steel drummers on TV.

"And as for the New Kids, they're just about the most famous rock group in the country. These entertainment people seem to work as hard as, well, as hard as the doctors and nurses at Stacey's hospital."

"I know what you're trying to say, Allison." Mr. Holtz sighed. "But I just can't see it. The entertainment business is fine, I guess, but you need to do something important with your life. You know, something that *helps* people. That's what I like about your sister Stacey's career."

"Okay, Dad, but give it just one more look, okay?" said Stacey, taking her father's arm. "You promised we could check out this play, right?"

"Okay, okay. I promised. But I don't think any play is going to change my mind."

Stacey led Mr. Holtz over to where the New Kids were signing autographs. The woman in the island costume passed the quartet's top hat, collecting piles of contributions for the boy drummer. The hat was filling up fast when Mr. Holtz dropped in a five-dollar bill.

Still pretending to be her sister, Stacey introduced her father to Jonathan, Jordan, Danny, Donnie, and Joe. Mr. Holtz congratulated them for a job well done.

"I like the way you were kind to that young fellow," he said.

"A couple of gigs like this," said Joe, "and the Little Drummer Boy there can buy himself a real set of drums."

"Come on, guys," said Stacey. "We're gonna be late for that play. And I got us some pretty good seats, too."

The New Kids said goodbye to their musical friends and set off toward the theater. Suddenly Jordan told the others to go on ahead and he would catch up with them. He said he'd forgotten something and would be right back.

Danny turned to Jonathan. "I notice you and Jordan are, like, coolin' it with the Lady Allison, huh?"

"Like they say, Danny, the ball's in her court. I don't think we've cooled anything. At least, I haven't. But we've gotta stop our riffin', am I right?"

"One million percent," Danny agreed.

After a few minutes Jordan ran up to the others, puffing to catch his breath. He was wearing only a light vest over his shirt.

Jonathan looked at his brother and smiled. He slowed his walk to keep pace with Jordan as the rest of the group moved ahead.

"Lose somethin', bro?" Jonathan asked.

"Huh?" said Jordan. "Oh, you mean that old leather jacket? Yeah. You know, Jon, it just wasn't the same after that taxi driver splashed it all up."

"No way." Jonathan smiled.

"Besides, the little guy needs that jacket a lot worse than I do. He was freezin'."

"And you, brother," said Jonathan, putting his arm around Jordan, "are chillin'."

Walking just ahead of the Knight brothers were Stacey and Mr. Holtz. They heard every word. Stacey looked up at her father as if to ask, See? What did I tell you?

Chapter

10

THE PLAY WAS ABOUT a young man named Steve whose father was an alcoholic. By the end of the first act all the New Kids were completely wrapped up in the story.

The theater was very small. During intermission the audience went outside. In the cold night air they stood around, sipping on sodas and talking about the play. Jonathan and Donnie disagreed over the character Steve and the cause of his problems.

"It was his father who caused all those bad things to happen," said Donnie. "Steve was born a loser."

"I don't think so," Jonathan remarked. "You've gotta stand on your own two feet. You can't just automatically let your parents' problems become *your* problems."

Jordan broke in. "Steve's got a way out," he said. "Don't forget Jennifer."

"They've been talking about this girl Jennifer for the whole play," Donnie protested. "But we still haven't seen her."

"You will," said Stacey, joining the conversation unexpectedly. "That is, I mean, I *think* you will."

Mr. Holtz had his theater program in his jacket pocket. He got it out to look up the name of the actress who would play the role of Jennifer.

"It says here that Jennifer is played by Constance Matthews. Ever hear of her, Allison?" Mr. Holtz still did not suspect his daughters had pulled a switch on him.

"No," said Stacey. "But, um, I heard somebody say they had a new girl in that part tonight. They just didn't have time to change it in the program."

A buzzer went off, signaling the end of intermission. As the audience returned to their seats, Stacey took her father's arm.

"You know, Dad," she said, "a play like this can get people talking about their own real-life problems. Sometimes people who have those problems might see themselves in the characters onstage. That could make them get help. Maybe a play like this could even keep some people out of hospitals."

"I guess so," Mr. Holtz agreed, somewhat reluctantly.

"Maybe that means an actress can help people just as much as a nurse can, you know?"

"Maybe," said her father. "But to make that kind of difference, you've got to be a really good actress, Allison. That takes years of training. You don't just step out on a stage and get people to believe you."

Stacey did not respond. She could only hope her father would be proven wrong.

The lights came up for the second act. After ten minutes went by the character of Jennifer appeared. She wore a flowing white gown under blue lights. She was very pale, with cascades of blond hair and dark red lips. With her very first lines

Jennifer became the strongest force on the stage.

Stacey leaned over and whispered, "Isn't she terrific, Dad?"

Mr. Holtz only nodded. He seemed hypnotized by the talented young actress on the stage. She moved around like a dancer, and when she spoke her lines, everyone in the little theater sat silently.

The New Kids sat spellbound in their seats. Each of them felt as though he were in a living room somewhere, sharing a secret moment with a troubled man and his family. It was a feeling they never got from watching television.

The play ended and the curtains came down on the stage. For a moment the audience sat still in the darkness. Finally it burst into applause, and the lights came up again for the actors to take their bows.

First came the supporting players, then the three people who played lesser roles. Then it was Jennifer's turn for a curtain call.

As the girl in the flowing white robe came onstage, the applauding people jumped to their feet. The New Kids were clapping loudest of all. Joe McIntyre couldn't resist stomping his feet and giving a little whoop-whoop!

And then the actress who played Jennifer reached up and pulled off her blond wig. When she rose from her bow to face the audience, she was a different person.

"Allison!" shouted three voices together. The voices belonged to Jonathan and Jordan Knight and to Mr. Holtz.

"Impossible," said Danny, putting his arm around Stacey. "Allison's right here."

Still applauding wildly, Mr. Holtz turned to the New Kids with a wide grin on his face. "Boys," he said, "I'm afraid we've all been tricked and tricked good. Meet Allison's twin sister, Stacey!"

"Twins!" shouted Jordan and Jonathan together.

"Whoa! That explains a lot," Danny said.

"You mean, that's really Allison onstage?" Jordan asked.

Jonathan turned to Stacey, his eyes wide with disbelief. "And you're *not* Allison?"

Stacey grinned as she continued to applaud for Allison and the other actors. "I hope you all aren't too mad. We never meant to come between brothers."

"This is unbelievable!" exclaimed Jon.

"Two sisters tricking two brothers!" Joe laughed. "That's pretty sensational."

Mr. Holtz leaned over and said, "You boys are just going to have to be twice as nice now, or my girls will be giving you double trouble."

"How about you, Daddy? Are you going to give *us* double trouble?"

Her father shook his head. "Sometimes it does take me a while, honey. But I'm not so old that I can't learn a thing or two. You and your sister have taught me a good lesson tonight."

"Then you'll let Allison be an actress?"

"Now I know I couldn't stop her if I tried. And I have a feeling she can do a lot more to help people out in the theater than she could in a hospital or an office building."

When most of the audience had left, the New Kids followed Stacey and Mr. Holtz up onto the little stage. Allison came out and tried to throw her arms around all of them at once.

"Did you like it?" she asked.

"You were great!" Jonathan said. Everyone else echoed his opinion. When the congratulations were over, at least for the moment, Jordan finally asked the question.

"So what's with this twin stuff?" he demanded.

"I couldn't help it," Allison said. "Remember all those phone calls yesterday morning? My agent was working on a last-minute callback audition. The girl who was supposed to take over the part of Jennifer wound up taking a different part. My agent was sure they were going to pick me instead."

"So, your agent was the guy who said you were *the only girl*, huh?" Danny asked.

"Sounds like someone was eavesdropping on a phone call," Stacey said.

"Hey, don't look at *me*," Danny protested. "I'm innocent."

"Anyway," Allison continued, "I had to ask Stacey to take my place for a while.

"That was me on the elephant, Jordan," Stacey explained. "And Jonathan, I was the one who rode with you on the zoo monorail."

"Whoa!" exclaimed Jordan.

"That explains a *lot*," said Jon.

"That also means you guys can stop fighting," Danny chimed in.

"What fighting?" Jordan asked.

"Not *us!*" Jonathan complained. The others groaned, and Jonathan couldn't stop himself from laughing. *"Hawr-hawr-hawr!"*

He gave Allison a hug, and Jordan put his arm around Stacey. *"Hawr-hawr-hawr!"* Jonathan laughed again. A camera flash went off, and they all saw stars in front of their eyes.

"Didn't even have to say *Gorgonzola,*" chirped the familiar voice of Monica Merriweather. "Everybody's laughing already."

"Hey," Donnie said, "it's Shaka and Monica."

"I thought we were finished with you *Teen Rhythm* people," said Joe.

"Not a chance," said Shaka. "Don't forget, Allison still works for us. That is, until she becomes a star. She told us you would all be here."

"Besides," said Monica, flashing her red braces, "we had to tell you to pick up a copy of *The New York Times* tomorrow. They're gonna run this picture."

Monica held up a black-and-white print for the boys to see. There was Jordan, trapped in the telephone booth by a horde of screaming fans. There were Joe and Donnie, peeking out from under the skirt of the Chinese dragon, about to pull Joe from the booth.

"Incredible!" said Jordan.

"You followed us after all?" asked Jonathan.

"For an ace photographer like Monica," Shaka said, smiling, "news is news. This one was too good to save for the magazine, so we rushed it to the newspaper."

"I hope you told them my brother was that ugly one in the front of the dragon," Jordan said.

"Absolutely," said Shaka. "The headline will read, 'New Kid Braves Dragon to Save Brother Knight!'"

"*Hawr-hawr-hawr!*" roared Jonathan. "Maybe we can find that dragon and make it part of our act tomorrow night."

"Great idea," said Danny, "as long as the two Knight brothers have *their* act back together."

"Chill, Danny," said Donnie. "Now that there are enough Holtz sisters to go around, the Knight brothers have nothing to fight about."

"Now how about some food?" suggested Allison. "I'm starving!"

"Pizza!" yelled Joe.

"I was thinking more like . . . the Russian Tea Room," said Allison.

Jonathan looked at Jordan and winked. "I think we can agree on that," he said.

"But we can't stay out too late," Allison cautioned. "You guys have a big show to do tomorrow night."

Mr. Holtz smiled and wrapped his arm around Allison. "So do you," he said. "A very big show. Can you get me another ticket?"